David
Webb

HARPY

COVEN: BOOK 1

DAVID NETH

DN Publishing

Harpy
Coven, Book 1
Copyright © 2021 by David Neth
Batavia, NY

www.DavidNethBooks.com

ISBN: 978-1-945336-09-6
First Edition

Subscribe to the author's newsletter for updates and exclusive content:
DavidNethBooks.com/Newsletter

Follow the author at:
www.facebook.com/DavidNethBooks
www.instagram.com/DavidNethBooks

Also by David Neth

Coven
Harpy
Siren
Valkyrie
Shapeshifter
Sorcerer
Enchantress

Under the Moon
The Full Moon
The Harvest Moon
The Blood Moon
The Crescent Moon
The Blue Moon

The Art of Magic

Fuse
Origin
Omertá
Oblivion

Heat
Black Magnet
Dust Storm
The Gatekeeper

Standalone
All I Ever Wanted

CHAPTER 1

- JUNE 1988 -

W hat are you going to do today?" Samantha smoothed out the hair on the sides of her head and inspected herself in the mirror. The room was a haze of hairspray and perfume.

"Running a few errands," Kathy replied from her spot at the end of her sister's bed.

"Applying to jobs?" Samantha pumped lotion into her hands and rubbed them together.

"Yes, I've got a list. I'm also going to run and get some more milk and bread, since we're out."

"Good," Samantha said. "There should be enough in the account to cover it."

"I actually have cash."

HARPY

"From where?"

"I found it in my dresser," Kathy said. "Apparently I had an emergency stash I forgot about."

Samantha studied her as she finished rubbing in the lotion. She didn't like the idea of Kathy using her life savings on last-minute groceries, but they didn't really have a choice. They were short on cash. Hence, the job interview she was about to go to. Rather, the *second* job interview. The first one earlier in the week went swimmingly, which only made her nerves for the second one worse.

"You could finish those dishes in the sink, too." Samantha grabbed a comb and a mini bottle of hair spray from her dresser and stepped out of the room to descend the stairs.

"That's on my list too." Kathy followed behind. "Are you sure you want me to get a job? How else would we get all this housework done?"

Samantha stopped in her path to her purse and shot her sister a look. "We'd manage."

Collecting the copies of her résumé and the other important papers she needed for her meeting, Samantha stuffed them in an envelope and hooked them under her arm as she threw her comb and hairspray into her purse.

She had another interview with Darius Wilcox, CPA, an accounting firm downtown. One of her former professors recommended the firm to her just before she graduated with her degree in accounting last month. It was the perfect fit and something she and Kathy desperately needed.

Samantha snatched up her keys, slung her purse over her shoulder and turned to her sister. "How do I look?"

"Very professional." Kathy beamed. "You're going to knock 'em dead! Again."

"I don't look like a wannabe college graduate?"

"No offense, but you *are* a college graduate," Kathy said. "And until someone gives you an opportunity to actually do something with it, you'll always be a wannabe."

Samantha rolled her eyes. "That's not encouraging."

"You look great, Sam. They already love you, which is why they called you back for another interview."

"Thanks."

"But, rest assured, it's certainly clear that you're the *older* sister."

Samantha rolled her eyes and pushed at Kathy's shoulder. "Yeah, and you wouldn't think one year would make that big of a difference, but here we are."

"Hey!" Kathy laughed. "What does that mean?"

"I don't have time for this. I'm going to be late."

"You have plenty of time. Good luck and knock 'em dead!"

"Let's hope it doesn't come to that," Samantha said with a smirk.

CHAPTER 2

Well, Miss Walker, you certainly have a lot to offer." Mr. Marsden offered a genuine smile and indicated Samantha's résumé and the notes he made through the interview. They were sitting at the end of the long conference table in one of the board rooms in the office suite. "Believe me, I don't tell everyone this, but you're one of our strongest candidates."

Samantha smiled. "Thank you. I've done my best to get as much experience as possible."

"I can see that." He fixed his tie and smoothed it down against his belly. "For the sake of clarity, I just like to explain the process. Typically when we take on new hires, we have them go through three rounds of interviews. We're pretty much done with the second round here. The third round—which you'll be moving on to—will consist of myself and a few other people from the firm as sort of a panel interview. From there, we'll give you a call with our decision, no matter what we choose. In all honesty, I still need to figure out who exactly is going to be on this panel, so there's some details on our side that still need to be worked out."

She nodded. "Okay. That sounds fair. Thank you for seeing me again today."

"Absolutely, thanks for coming down." He stood and came around the table and extended his hand. "It was nice to see you again. Take care and we'll be in touch."

Samantha shook his hand and thanked him again before exiting the office.

Down in the lobby, she dug some spare change from the bottom of her purse and fed it into a free payphone, among the long line of them. When she heard the dial tone, she dialed the house and waited for her sister to pick up, hoping Kathy was back already from her errands.

Samantha needed to tell someone the good news right away and her boyfriend Steven was at work at a different accounting firm. Kathy was the only one she knew would be free.

"Hello?" Kathy answered on the last ring.

"It's me."

"Oh! How'd it go? Did you get the job?"

"Not yet, but it's looking that way," she said. "He told me I'm moving on to the next round."

"The next round?"

"Yeah, the next round of interviews."

"Geez, how many rounds are there?" Kathy asked. "It feels like you've been interviewing there forever."

"It's been two interviews."

"Well, is this next one the last one?"

"Should be." Samantha swatted at the air. The man two payphones down was smoking. She wished they would make it illegal to smoke indoors. She hated breathing it in. "Anyway, I called because I thought we should celebrate. Do you want to go to lunch?"

"Sure! But aren't we tight on money?"

"I'm about to have a new job."

Kathy laughed. Samantha was usually the one who didn't count on anything until it was a sure thing, so the fact that Samantha herself was predicting landing this job was a statement.

"Okay," Kathy said with a chuckle. "You heading out now?"

"Yeah, I should be there to pick you up in about fifteen minutes. Be ready."

"I'm on it, boss."

CHAPTER 3

Mark Gad tapped his pen on the updated privacy policy packet in front of him. It was marked up with notes and doodles he made during the meeting, which was still dragging on.

He looked up at the clock and saw that it was 11:57. His stomach growled, but most of all he was craving a cigarette. He finished his last one just before the meeting at his desk. The fact that several of his coworkers sitting around the conference table were puffing on their own smokes made his craving worse.

Finally, Mr. Bellman, the Senior VP of Communications at Blue Water Insurance, announced that the meeting was adjourned and every man seated around the conference table shot to his feet and rushed to the door to start their lunch break.

HARPY

Mark tossed his packet on his desk in the cubicle space the higher-ups had the audacity to call his office. He grabbed his keys, wallet, and ID, and walked through the makeshift hallway around other cubicle "offices" to the lobby, where he stood amongst other workers waiting for the elevator to take them down.

When the doors opened, everyone crammed into the elevator, invading personal space and pretending like it wasn't a problem. Acting like this behavior was perfectly normal. The sad part was that it had become the lunchtime routine now that the weather broke. Everyone was desperate to get outside and enjoy the sunshine, even if only for thirty minutes a day.

Once he got out onto the sidewalk, Mark stepped into the small hole-in-the-wall convenience store in the corner storefront of his office building. It was quiet in there and he relished in the silence as he browsed the shelves for something to snack on for lunch—he forgot his leftovers at home.

Opening the refrigerator in the back of the store, Mark pulled out a box of Hot Pockets and reached for a bottle of Cherry 7UP from the top shelf. He brought his goodies to the counter and told the cashier he wanted a pack of Marlboros.

After he paid, Mark stepped out on the street, dug through the plastic bag, and retrieved his cigarettes. He opened the celofane, tapped out a smoke, and brought it to his mouth to light it.

Finally satisfied now that he had a good drag, Mark himself

started to enjoy the beautiful weather they were having. Cloudless sky, people passing by on the sidewalk, cars whizzing by on the street with the windows down. Summer weather was here for the season.

With the plastic bag digging into his palm from the heavy 7UP bottle, Mark set it on the sidewalk next to the building until he finished his cigarette. He slipped the pack into his pocket and took another look up at the beautiful blue sky.

To his right, he caught of glimpse of three birds flying through the air further down State Street. As if sensing him looking, they turned and started their direction up the street, growing larger as they approached.

Mark's smoke clung to his bottom lip as he stared up at the trio in confusion, mouth hung slack. Now that they were closer and he had a good look at them, the birds looked different. Almost with a *human* face. And they looked to be about the size of a regular person. Worse, they seemed to be charging toward him.

Turning, he tossed his cigarette on the ground and moved toward the door to the office building, not wanting to risk stopped to pick up what he bought for lunch.

The birds swung low, swiping at Mark's arm as he grabbed the door handle to the office building. He ducked out of the way before they could attack him again, but now they were blocking his way into the building.

One of them looped through the air and looked to be

winding up to take another shot, but Mark wasn't going to risk it. He broke into a run down the sidewalk with the three birds hot in pursuit.

CHAPTER 4

You certainly sound excited about this job, but it sounds dreadfully boring to me." Kathy sat back in her seat and popped a French fry in her mouth.

The sisters had a seat outdoor on the sidewalk at a pub on State Street in downtown Erie. The gentle breeze offered relief to the otherwise hot day. More than once, Samantha wished she had stopped at the house long enough to change, but if that were the case, her rationality that they didn't have much money would've kicked in and she would've opted to not go to lunch. This moment deserved a celebration.

"We are two very different people," Samantha replied.

"With one very similar trait."

Their magic. Both sisters loved being witches, but only

Harpy

Samantha felt continuously inconvenienced by it…and equally obligated to use her powers to help people. It was a double-edged sword, being a witch.

Samantha never liked even alluding to their magic in public, so Kathy quickly changed the subject.

"I applied to three jobs today and I'm going to go back to another place tomorrow to talk to the manager about getting an application."

"Where'd you apply?"

"Woolworth's, Grant's—I'm going to go back to this diner place tomorrow. I guess they need another waitress."

"Waitressing? And cashiering? Kathy, don't you want something more stable?"

She shrugged. "Maybe, but when Jeremy and I get married it won't really matter, will it?"

"That is incredibly short-sighted."

"Well, if you're making me choose between slaving away for a career or enjoying my life as it is, I pick living my life the way I want. Now, if I've been relieved of my Cinderella duty for the day, I'd like to ask your permission to see my boyfriend for our date this afternoon."

Samantha shot her a look. "My permission?"

"I mean, you've been bossing me around a bit, haven't you? Do you not like it because it has a ring of truth to it?" She hooked an eyebrow and gave her sister a smirk.

"Holding you to a higher standard and expecting you to

pull your weight around the house when you don't have a job does not make me a slave-driver."

"No, it makes you a mother and you are certainly not mine."

"Anyway..." Samantha drew out the word. "You can see Jeremy whenever you want. Just don't marry him so I get off your back about getting a job. Whether or not there's a ring on your finger, I still want the best for you."

"And I love you for that, but I'm good." Kathy pushed her plate back. "Besides, I think you deserve some quality time with your boo."

"My boo?"

"Steven. You two have been going together for a couple years."

"So have you and Jeremy," Samantha fired back. "That is, if we're not counting the breakups."

"We don't break up, we take breaks," Kathy clarified. "And we're talking about you right now."

"No, *you're* talking about me." Samantha waved down the waitress. "I'm trying to get out of this conversation because I know where it's going."

"Come on!" Kathy nagged. "Even you have to admit that you think a proposal is coming."

The waitress came and handed Samantha the check and collected their plates.

When she was gone, Samantha pulled money out of her wallet and said, "Just because you want me to get engaged for some reason doesn't mean it's going to happen. Steven and I are just—we're good. Just as we are for now."

"But *soon*—"

"I don't know." Samantha said with finality. She closed her wallet and stuck it back in her purse. "Are you ready?"

"Yep."

When they stood to walk around the gate separating the eating area from the sidewalk, they were nearly hit by a man running by. He wore a tie over his white button-down shirt that was coming untucked from his black pants.

Strange.

Samantha and Kathy exchanged glances with each other and watched the man run right through the crosswalk at the end of the block without stopping. Cars honked as they swerved to miss him. Cuss words erupted from their open windows.

Moments later, Kathy noticed three large birds swooping by them overhead. Except, something was off about them. She nudged her sister and pointed.

Without a word, both of them took off in a run in pursuit of the man and the strange bird creatures. Their boyfriends would have to wait. They needed to be witches right now.

CHAPTER 5

Pumping their legs as they dashed down the street, Samantha and Kathy raced to catch up to the man and his predators.

Samantha lagged behind her sister since she was still dressed in the heels she wore to her interview. Her toes squished at the end of each shoe where the fabric dug into her flesh. She did her best to ignore it, running on the tips of her toes to keep from breaking the heel. That would only add insult to injury.

"This way!" Kathy called back to her sister as she pointed to a building around the corner.

With aching feet, Samantha followed until she rounded the corner and caught a glimpse of her sister dart into the entrance of the parking garage on French Street. Groaning, she followed

HARPY

Kathy inside several seconds later.

As soon as she cleared the entrance into the concrete structure, she heard the echoes of the man's screams and the screeches of the birds.

"Kathy!"

"Almost there!"

Samantha watched as her sister rounded the corner onto the second level. Shouts and screeches erupted louder than ever, just out of view.

"Leave him alone!" Kathy shouted.

Samantha rounded the corner and saw three bird-women leaning toward a black SUV, all turned to look back at Kathy.

Each of them had feathered wings sticking out of their backs, despite otherwise looking like regular women from the waist up. Their legs were skinny and covered in the same scale-like skin most fowls had, which led down to their clawed toes. Feathers covered them from their elbows down to the talons that replaced their hands.

All three looked at the sisters with venom in their eyes and the one in the middle let out a loud screech that echoed in the concrete cavern and forced the sisters to bring their hands to their ears.

While distracted, the flock of bird-women swept in to attack the witches, knocking them both to the ground before either of them could use their powers.

Kathy tried to push away as two of them swatted their sharp

claws at her, scraping up her forearms as she fought. She gave in and decided to protect her face instead and roll away from them, but one of them waved her talon at Kathy and a strong gust of wind pinned her to the floor until the bird-woman's foot could hold her there.

Samantha struggled to break free under her attacker. After swatting and squirming, she finally brought one leg up and extended it upward as hard as she could, driving her stiletto heel into the fowl's chest. The bird-woman screeched again, but backed off to nurse her wounds a safe distance away.

Springing up to her feet, Samantha turned her attention to the two women pinning Kathy to the floor. Sending another kick at one of them, she managed to equal the playing field, so each witch only faced one creature.

Freed of one of the creatures, Kathy brought her hands up and used her magic on the second one attacking her to freeze her in time. Kathy scurried out from beneath her. Once she was back on her feet, she delivered a hard swing kick straight at the bird-woman, who unfroze and skidded across the floor against a nearby car.

Samantha followed suit with her own swing kick and both witches took a protective stance in front of the man who cowered behind the black SUV.

The three bird-women recollected in front of the witches, each of them cradling their respective injuries. Samantha and Kathy both tried not to pay any attention to theirs, although both women's arms were bleeding.

Finally, the flock of birds let out a collective screeches and took a running start out of the parking garage, where they soared into the air and away from their prey.

With heaving breaths, Samantha and Kathy exchanged glances with each other and then turned back to the man, who crouched near the front of the SUV gasping for breath with tears in his eyes.

CHAPTER 6

- APRIL 1953 -

It was growing dark by time Sharon and Patrick brought up the rest of their boxes from the moving truck downstairs. Even with the cool temperatures, carrying furniture and boxes up three flights of stairs by themselves was hard work. They were both sweaty and tired by time everything was finally in the apartment.

"Well, that's everything," Patrick said as he put an arm around his new wife. His dark blue T-shirt clung to his sweaty chest, but Sharon leaned into him regardless.

"Now to unpack," she said.

"This is the start of the new chapter of our lives," he said. "We're married, we have a new city to call home, and I have a job lined up. We're going to get our start here, Sharon. I can feel it."

HARPY

Their new home was in Washington, Pennsylvania, less than thirty miles southwest of Pittsburgh. It was a small city that still offered some of the amenities of a larger town. Still, the newlyweds took advantage of their move from Scranton, Pennsylvania, by securing a prime apartment on Main Street in Washington. Real estate was more expensive in Scranton than Washington, so they were able to afford a higher-end apartment in their new city. They were right across from the county courthouse.

Sharon wrapped her arms around her new husband and hugged him tight. "This is our home."

"Yeah, but we're running low on daylight now," Patrick said, pulling away from her. "Why don't you get started unpacking these boxes—I'd suggest finding the lamps first." He smirked at her. The apartment didn't have overhead lighting. "I'm going to go take the truck back to the rental place. I'll help when I get back."

She smiled and kissed him. "Okay, dear. Drive safe."

As Patrick disappeared out the door and down the staircase that they had traveled up that day more times than they could count, Sharon turned to the boxes and began trying to sort them out.

They did their best to organize what rooms the boxes belonged to when they moved, but the apartment was mostly a large open space. The only separate rooms were the bedroom and the bathroom, tucked around the corner from the staircase

22

at the front of the building.

Still, she set to work, straightening out tables, pulling out the lamps to illuminate the room as the sunlight continued to fade, and unpacking the boxes of things they'd need sooner than later. Dishes and silverware, linens for the bedroom and bathroom, and, of course, Patrick's radio, which he liked to listen to every night.

As she worked, Sharon used what little magic she had, and created a small breeze in the apartment to cool her off, despite the windows all being closed. They were painted shut and would take a little finessing by her husband to get working.

Sharon didn't like to use her magic often. She saw no use for it since her goals in life were to be a housewife and eventually a mother. Sure, there were women who were going to college and working, but Sharon liked the idea of taking care of the home, which didn't require her to use her magic.

And Patrick agreed. He knew she was a witch and didn't seem bothered by it, which she guessed was because she never practiced witchcraft. It remained a secret between the two of them and she felt it added a hint of mystery and intrigue to their relationship.

He had confirmed her thoughts when he told her that it was best to not use her magic so they could keep it a secret. It took a lot for her to learn to stifle it. She had been so used to feeling the wind kick up whenever she got mad or overly excited. But she knew Patrick had a point, so she bottled up her magic even more than she usually did because that's what her husband wanted and as a doting housewife, she needed to keep him happy.

The apartment was starting to look more and more like a home and Sharon was proud of the way it was shaping up. She jotted down a list of things they would need to get to finish furnishing the place: curtains for the windows overlooking Main Street; more lamps, preferably standing ones because they didn't have very many tables; and some area rugs to cover the worn spots on the hardwood floors. She could get some of those when she ventured into town once Patrick started working at the garage.

When Sharon heard the footsteps of her husband coming up the stairs, she quickly tried to wrangle as much of the packing clutter to one corner so the apartment appeared more presentable.

Patrick stepped into the apartment with his head down and tossed his keys on the table beside the door. "That bastard ripped me off! Charged me an extra ten cents a mile because the gas tank was below half!"

"Oh, I'm sorry, dear," Sharon cooed. "But look! Doesn't the apartment look great?" She smiled and opened her arms to showcase the room.

"It's nice, sweetheart," he said quickly before moving on to his next question. "What did you make for dinner?"

"Dinner?" Her face dropped, only slightly so as not to

disappoint her new husband.

"Yeah, I'm hungry. It's been a long day."

She brought her hands together and fiddled with her nails. "I, uh—well, I spent so much time working on getting things organized that I didn't have time to make—"

"You didn't make me dinner?" His voice was low, almost threatening.

"Sweetie, we don't even have very much to eat," she said. "I was planning on running to the grocery store tomorrow—"

"That doesn't help me now!" he yelled. "What am I supposed to eat now?"

Sharon swallowed the lump in her throat. "We can order a pizza." She reached for the phone.

"We don't have extra money to spend on pizza because *you* didn't think ahead," he snapped at her and snatched the phone from her grasp.

She raised a shaking hand and backpedaled to the kitchen. The air in the room began to shift, as if there was a draft. She hoped that's all Patrick would chalk it up to. "I think we have some canned goods. I can make us a couple of tuna fish sandwiches, how's that?"

He grumbled and sank onto the couch, throwing his feet up on a nearby box. "I suppose it better than nothing."

"Okay, I'll hurry." She disappeared into the kitchen and fished out four slices of bread with shaking hands. The whole time, she tried to calm herself down.

HARPY

He just had a bad day. He's not mad at you, you're just the one who's here. This is what a marriage looks like.

Except, deep in her gut, she knew this wasn't what a marriage was supposed to be. But she was too scared to even think it, let alone say anything to her husband. They were married now. She made her choice. And that was that.

Besides, it's not like he hit her or anything. He just had a bad day.

CHAPTER 7

I get it that he was just the target of an attack by some strange creatures and he needs time to process, but can't I freeze him again?" Kathy murmured to her sister under the wails of sobs erupting from the man in the next room. She was bandaging up Samantha's arm after having her own wrapped up as well.

They were back at the house and the man hadn't stopped sobbing and hyperventilating since the parking garage. Despite offers to help him calm down, he was inconsolable and the sisters gave up on trying to help him. He would need to get a grip on his own.

"The last thing we need is to equip him with even more questions." Samantha winced as Kathy applied a special ointment to her wound. A recipe they found in *The Art of Magic*,

27

their magic book that had been in the family for generations. "He's already seen his fair share of oddities today, so we can only hope he missed your use of magic."

"You say that as if it was my fault." Kathy carefully applied the bandage over the wound.

"No, of course you didn't have a choice, but—" Samantha winced again. "Let's just hope he hasn't seen anything that could be incriminating to us."

Kathy smoothed out the adhesive of the bandage. "We didn't do anything incriminating."

"You know what I mean." Samantha pulled her arm back and gently rubbed the wound through the wrapping. "What we need to do is get some answers."

"I haven't looked them up in the book yet, but those creatures reminded me of a harpy or something, right?"

Samantha nodded. "That's what I was thinking too. We'll have to double check, but from what I remember, they only go after people who have done something bad."

"So you're thinking this guy isn't so innocent after all?"

A loud sob—possibly a forced one—prevented Samantha from immediately responding.

"I'm just saying we need answers before we make our next move."

"Would it be wrong to slip him a little potion to get him to talk? Or, at the very least, get him to calm down?"

"That's if he'll even take it."

Kathy crossed her arms, but felt the sting of pain and let them drop again. "It's worth a shot."

"Maybe we should try talking to him first."

"I tried in the car," Kathy said. "It didn't work. And if *I* couldn't get him to talk…"

Samantha shot her a look at the jab. "Very funny."

"Honestly, though, what makes you think he's going to talk on his own?"

"It's worth a shot. You tried talking to him when he was still in shock from it all."

Another sob echoed throughout the house.

"And you're saying he's no longer in shock?" Kathy asked.

Samatha sighed. "Let me try again. If he doesn't talk, then we'll resort to magic."

"Okay."

"In the meantime, check the book and see if you can find anything about those women and what they want. Hopefully we can figure out a game plan from there. I just don't want them to get the chance to hurt anyone else."

Kathy shook her head. "Me neither. I'll see what I can find."

The sisters turned to get to work, but the ringing doorbell stopped them both in their tracks. Even the man's whimpers subsided.

"Who's that?" Samantha asked.

Kathy shrugged.

Still jittery from the attack in the parking garage, Samantha

HARPY

opened the front door slowly at first until she saw Jeremy standing on the other side. Even when she opened it, she stood in front of the opening to prevent him from walking inside. She didn't want to explain why there was a crying man in their living room. No plausible explanation came to mind at the moment.

"Jeremy, what are you doing here?" Kathy walked up beside her sister.

"Picking you up for our date." He stepped forward and kissed Kathy. "We said this afternoon, right?"

CHAPTER 8

That was supposed to be later." Kathy cast Jeremy a look with a furrowed brow.

"Well, I got out of class early and thought we could get a jump start." Jeremy was finishing up his last year at Penn State Behrend, which was just outside of Erie. He had flunked a semester and was taking those classes over again whenever he could, which meant he was currently enrolled in a twelve-week summer class that lasted from May to August. "I didn't think you had anything pressing going on."

Samantha cleared her throat, but Kathy ignored her.

"Uh…nothing that my sister can't handle on her own."

Samantha cleared her throat again, louder this time. Kathy elbowed her and then winced as the scratch from the attack was irritated.

Jeremy noticed her bandage. "What happened to your arm?"

"Oh, she fell," Samantha cut in. She pushed her sister back and said, "Look, now's not—"

"And your arm too?" he asked.

"Leaned against the hood of my car and burned myself," she lied. "The sun's been brutal this week."

"I didn't think it was too bad," he said.

"So!" Kathy said quickly. "Our date, yes. We'd better get going."

Samantha caught her sister's arm. "Um, Kathy, I actually need your help with something before you get going."

Kathy glared at her sister and muttered through gritted teeth, "Okay." Turning, her expression changed to a friendly smile. "Sweetie, why don't you go take a seat in the next room? Samantha and I need to discuss some things…apparently."

Jeremy nodded and stepped past them into the living room. Kathy cringed when she heard him say, "Oh, hi. Who are you?" to the man whimpering on the couch. His cries may have subsided long enough for their conversation at the door, but she completely blanked when she invited Jeremy in.

"Good luck explaining that," Samantha whispered.

Kathy grabbed her sister's good arm and pulled her into the kitchen. "I'll come up with something."

"Uh, you think? Are you seriously still going on your date?"

"What am I supposed to do? Blow him off without a perfectly good reason just so I can read a passage in the book?"

"So instead you're going to leave me here alone with a strange man who is a target for some reason we haven't even figured out yet. Kathy, there are still too many unknowns."

"All right, well, think about it. The harpies—or whatever they are—were hurt when we stopped them from killing that guy. They're going to need to regroup and think of another plan of attack before they come for him again. We have time."

"How do you know they're not fast healers?" Samantha countered. "How do you know they even need a long time to regroup? Maybe they'll send more. The fact is, they traveled in a pack so there might be another group that could come in and take him. Are you going to leave me alone with that possibility?"

Kathy tilted her head down and gave her sister a look. "I thought we weren't going to live in paranoia?"

"This isn't—"

"You're trying to get me to stay based purely on speculation. We need answers, but we also need to live our lives. I can't just blow off Jeremy when there isn't an imminent threat. Take the time while I'm gone to talk to this guy—learn his *name*—and try to get some sort of explanation out of him as to why he might be under attack. The best lead we have right now is currently sitting in the living room talking to my boyfriend."

HARPY

The same thought struck both of them at once and they stared at each other in worry before they both darted back to the living room.

"Jeremy, I'm ready now," Kathy announced louder than usual. She didn't want the man to say anything to Jeremy that might indicate the sisters were witches—or even that they knew anything more than the nonmagical. According to Jeremy and the rest of the world, there were no such things as witches.

"Oh, I was just talking to your friend Mark." He stood and met Kathy by the front door. "He said he might be interested in offering me a job when I graduate."

Kathy and Samantha both looked between the two men.

"Oh, that's...nice," Kathy said with as much enthusiasm as she could muster at the moment. "Anyway, where are we going on our date?" She did her best to lead him toward the door.

"See you later, Mark," Jeremy said with his arm slung over Kathy's shoulder, who was stepping to the front door. "I'll be in touch when I'm closer to graduation."

Mark gave a thumbs up. "You got it, buddy."

"Okay then!" Samantha said. "No reason to stick around here any longer. Have fun, you two!"

Graciously, the front door closed and Kathy and Jeremy were gone.

Samantha sat on the arm of the oversized chair across the room from Mark. "So, I see you've calmed down quite a bit."

34

He took a deep breath. "The shock of it has worn off, I suppose."

"Still, it was a pretty traumatic thing you went through."

"Yeah, but now it's over."

Samantha noted that there was no "thank you."

"So, your name is Mark?"

"Yup. And yours is…?"

"Samantha," she said. "Do you have a last name?"

He narrowed his eyes. "Who are you?"

She forced a laugh to lighten the mood. The tension was building regardless. "I'm Samantha. Walker is my last name, if you're curious."

"Well, Samantha Walker, I would like to go home now."

"Just a minute. I have a few questions first. Do you have any idea why those…*creatures* were after you?"

He shrugged and turned up his hands. "No idea."

"You didn't do anything that might upset them?"

"I was at work, went down to the corner store to buy some lunch and a pack of cigarettes, and then they started running after me." He ran his hands through his stubbly hair. "Oh shoot, I need to call the office. They're going to dock me for an extended lunch! I need to get back there!"

"Mark, relax. I'll take you wherever you want to go, I just need some answers first."

"No, I need to get out of here." He stood and stepped to the door.

HARPY

"Mark, wait!" Staring into his eyes, she used her mind specialty to lace her words with persuasion. "Mark, wouldn't you like to tell me a little more about yourself?"

"I…uh…I'm Mark Gad. Senior Accounts Manager at Blue Water Insurance. My wife's name is Tina, but…but…"

He seemed to be fighting the persuasion, but Samantha relented.

"What about your wife, Mark? What are you trying to tell me? You can say whatever you want to me. It's okay. I won't tell."

"I've been seeing someone else," he admitted. "Or, I was."

"What's her name?"

"I don't want to say."

"Come on, it's okay."

Mark was fighting her magic hard and doubt crept into Samantha's thoughts so much that the effects of her magic wore off.

He shook his head. "I'd really like to leave now."

Disappointed, she nodded. "Okay. Let's go."

She grabbed her keys from her purse and followed him out the door to her car.

"You said you want to go back to the office?" She climbed in and started the car, turning in her seat to look out the back window as she backed down the driveway.

"Yeah."

"You said it's Blue Water Insurance? Where's that?"

"State and 10th."

36

He wasn't saying much anymore. Probably because he realized he said more than he intended. After what he saw in the parking garage, he likely questioned everything that had happened, especially related to Samantha and Kathy.

Still, Samantha was determined to get further answers out of him. Her power usually required some kind of connection, which could typically be accomplished by looking someone in the eyes. Something she couldn't do while she was driving.

Turning off of Cherry Street to West 38th, Samantha pushed her persuasion power again.

"There wasn't anything bad that you did that would make those creatures chase you down, was there?"

Mark was quiet. His eyes focused straight ahead, watching the traffic move between the lanes on the road ahead of them.

"It's just, when we got there it seemed like they wanted to kill you and I can't imagine they would do that unless there was a good reason."

Silence.

So this was Mark's new strategy. He knew that when she questioned him at the house he said more than he intended so instead he was going to stay quiet.

The rest of the ride downtown was uncomfortable and awkward until Samantha pulled up in front of Mark's office building.

"Before you go, I want to at least get your contact information in case they come after you again," she said.

HARPY

"I know where you live. I'll find you."

She reached for his arm. "Wait."

He looked down at her hand and then gave her a nasty look. "I know you and your sister know more than you let on. I *saw* the way you two fought them. I saw what your sister did to those creatures. Now, unless you want me to contact the *Erie Times-News* about my story of what happened, I suggest you let me go and leave me alone." He pulled his arm away from her grasp and stepped out of the car.

"Mark!" she called for him.

"We don't know each other, ma'am." He slammed the door and crouched down into the window. "And I'd prefer to keep it that way."

CHAPTER 9

- JULY 1953 -

Sharon sat on the window sill, with her feet on the metal fire escape off the back of their apartment. She fanned herself with her hand, stirring up a slight supernatural breeze to help cool her off. With the temperatures reaching over ninety degrees and the heat rising to their third floor apartment, she was burning up. The long list of chores she had been working on all day didn't help, either.

Giving up on even the supernatural breeze, which was only moving warm air, Sharon extended her feet and raised her arms in the air to stretch. Her back popped and her muscles tensed, but it was the first time she had sat down all day and it felt good to loosen up a bit.

Inside, she heard Patrick stomp up the stairs and she

quickly ducked back through the window, banging her head on the pane as she did. If he saw her on the fire escape and not inside working he'd be mad. To her, it was only fair that she have the house nice and tidy for him when he got home after putting in a long day at work. Especially in this heat.

The garage was supposed to have closed three hours ago, but sometimes he worked late to finish whatever it was he was working on that day. But then, he'd never been *this* late before.

Inside, she clutched her head where she smacked it and rushed to the kitchen to find something to make for dinner. Yet another night where she wasn't prepared for Patrick's arrival home. She needed to get a better handle on being a wife.

But then, she did have a lot to do and the idea of turning on the oven in this heat was outrageous to her. Especially since Patrick still hadn't fixed the painted-over windows. And how could she have dinner ready when Patrick was late getting home? It was now almost eight o'clock.

Patrick swung open the door and stepped in. "Sharon?"

She came around the corner from the kitchen, a head of lettuce in a bowl. She had ripped off a few leaves in an attempt to make it look like she hadn't forgotten about dinner.

"What have you been *doing* all day?" he scolded.

She looked around the apartment and saw the laundry draped over the furniture. There was some on the line out the back window, but the line wasn't long enough to hold everything. Patrick had told her to not use the dryer in order to

DAVID NETH

save on extra quarters, but that meant hang-drying everything.

And Patrick didn't like to look at it, so she usually tried to make sure everything was put away before he got home, but with cleaning all day and running to the market, she had only just pulled the clothes out of the washer in the basement before she took her break on the fire escape, so everything was still wet.

"This place is a mess!" he shouted.

She stepped closer, but stopped when she saw his hard expression. His eyes were bloodshot too and she could smell the alcohol wafting off of him. He was still wearing his coveralls from the garage—maybe he *had* been working late—which were covered in grease and grime.

"I'm sorry, dear," she said. "I've just had a lot to do today and it's been a very hot day—"

"You think I don't know how hot it is?" Patrick asked. "I've been working out in it all day!"

"Yes, I know," she said. "But I've been working too—"

"Doing what?" He motioned around the room. "This place doesn't look any cleaner than when I left it this morning!"

"Well, that's not true," she said. "I mopped and did the laundry and dusted—"

"Are you calling me a liar?"

"Of course not, honey," she said. "I'm just saying you're mistaken."

"And with all you've supposedly had to do, what do you have for me to eat?" He pointed to the head of lettuce in a bowl.

41

HARPY

"Just a salad? You ran to the market and that's all you got? What else are you spending my money on? I work hard for that money, you realize that, right?"

"There's food in the fridge," she said. "Here, why don't you sit down and I'll fix us something quick. I wasn't sure when you'd be home." She set the bowl down on the nearest surface and rushed to the couch, where Patrick usually liked to sit, and pulled one of his wet shirts off, looking for another place to hang it.

When she turned around, she watched as Patrick tossed the rest of the clothes laying on the couch on the floor.

"You could've at least hung these up," she muttered.

He kicked off his dirty boots, getting dried mud and gunk on the hardwood floors she spent all morning scrubbing. "Yeah, well, you should've timed your day better so the clothes would've been dry by now. You know I hate to see them draped all over everything."

Sharon bent over to pick up the clothes and saw grease smears all over them. "You didn't even wash your hands!" It was the first time in their entire relationship that she raised her voice with him. It must've been the heat that was getting to her. "These clothes are ruined! I don't even know if I can get the stain out."

Slowly, he leaned forward on his knees. "Excuse me? I come home from working all day to a house that hasn't been maintained and you have the audacity to yell at *me*?"

Sharon hung the clothes over the edge of a chair. "I told you, I've been working all day too. And this heat is not helping any. I'm hot, Patrick. And I'm tired. I don't think it's too much for me to ask you to wash your hands when you come home and to take off—" She bent over and snatched his boots up off the floor and carried them to the tray by the door. "—your *filthy* boots when you come home!" Feeling brave, she stepped in front of him— even as he rose to his feet—and pointed to the kitchen. "Now go wash your hands before you stain anything else in here and ruin *my* hard work!"

His eyes flared and before she could react, she felt the hot sting of his hand on her cheek and she collapsed to the floor, dispersing all of her bravery with the fall.

Clutching her cheek, she looked up at him with shock.

"Talk to me like that again and see what happens." He sat back on the couch and put his feet up. He got comfortable and stared up at the ceiling and crossed his arms.

"Honey, I'm sorry," she murmured in a quiet voice. "I didn't mean to yell at you, but—"

"I don't want to hear it," he said. "Go make us something for dinner. I'm hungry."

She gulped and looked at him, surprised at what just happened.

But it had only been one time.

And he *had* had a long day.

And she *should've* planned her day better.

43

HARPY

Still, her cheek felt as if it were on fire and beneath it all, she was embarrassed. When did Patrick become this person? Or was he just acting like this because she was a bad wife? Was this what marriage was?

Slowly picking herself off the floor, she quietly grabbed the bowl from where she had left it and returned to the kitchen to finish making her husband dinner. If nothing else, she owed him that after ruining his day like she had.

CHAPTER 10

Kathy and Jeremy laid together on the bed after they'd finished. It was only for a few minutes before Jeremy pulled away and swung his feet to the floor to get up.

"Where are you going?" Kathy asked.

He nodded to the door. "Super Mario Brothers. You wanna play?"

She rolled her eyes and turned to gather her things from beside his bed, pushing aside the opened bags of Lay's, Orville's, and several candy wrappers. For the most part, his room was tidy—well, for a college boy—but the remnants of his bedtime snacking was sometimes the reason their cuddle times were cut short. Kathy hated laying there breathing in the scents of a convenience store explosion.

45

HARPY

Today, however, Nintendo was to blame for ruining their cuddle time.

"What's the matter?" he asked.

"Was this your idea of a date?"

"What? We're spending time together. I offered to have you play."

And sometimes, Jeremy's behavior was the reason they didn't stay in bed and hold each other longer.

"Just forget it." She pulled on her jeans and smoothed out the wrinkles in her shirt. Jeremy sometimes made her feel like an accessory or a check-box on a to-do list. Quality time with girlfriend? Check!

Clad in his boxers, Jeremy stepped to her and hugged her. "Hey, look, I'm sorry we're not going to a fancy dinner or anything. I just can't afford it."

"I don't *need* a fancy dinner," she said.

"Then what is it?"

She looked at him, stared deep into his eyes and her heart melted. She was making a big deal out of nothing. They were young, broke, and in love. Spending time with each other was more than enough.

Kathy forced a smile. "Nothing. It's—I'll get over it."

"That's my girl." He kissed her and then pulled on the rest of his clothes before walking out to the main living area. "Come on, we can play teams."

"No thanks." She followed him out and sat beside him on

the couch, throwing her legs over his lap after he turned on the gaming console. "I'll just watch."

Jeremy pulled her legs closer to him and kissed the back of her hand, waiting for his game to load.

"Just promise me we'll do something fun this weekend," she said. "It doesn't have to cost anything. Maybe even just going to Presque Isle and walking around."

"Presque Isle?" He made a face. "It'll be packed on the weekend."

She shrugged. "It doesn't have to be there. Just…something."

"Sure, babe." He patted her legs. "I'll come up with something."

The game loaded and Kathy considered joining him as a second player. If Jeremy was going to indulge in what she wanted for their weekend date, she should indulge in what he wanted to do now. Except, before she got a chance to say anything, Jeremy selected single player and started the game without asking her again if she was sure.

Kathy watched him play for a while. This was essentially what most of their dates had been like lately. Even with Jeremy's summer classes, he never seemed to spend a lot of time doing homework.

But then, with Kathy running out with Samantha all the time to deal with magical emergencies, Jeremy could've been doing homework in that time. She didn't want to bring it to his attention that a woman with no job, no kids, and barely any responsibilities was often unavailable. Not that that didn't mean that Jeremy didn't notice.

Although she was bored watching Jeremy play his game, she knew that with his schedule, he tried to combine multiple things at once. Besides, even if Jeremy was playing a game, it didn't mean she couldn't talk to him.

"So how was class?" She studied her nails and tried not to show that she was overthinking everything.

"It was fine."

"Just fine?"

He made a face and his thumb clicked down on the controller, which distracted him for a few seconds before he responded, "Yeah."

"Did you get any homework?"

He sighed, his eyes still locked on the screen. "Not much. Just a quick little report I need to do before next week."

"That's good." She looked around for something else to talk about. This was harder than she thought.

Before she could think of another question, the door opened and a tall man with a tank top and jean shorts walked in. It was Michael, Jeremy's only remaining roommate after the semester ended the month before.

Kathy sat up straighter and pulled her legs closer to herself. Her boyfriend didn't seem to pay too much attention to her withdrawal.

DAVID NETH

Jeremy's dad paid for his townhouse in Lawrence Park, just north of Erie. It was nice, kind of small for the four guys who lived here during the semester. Despite the various parties they'd had nearly every weekend all year, Jeremy and Michael were the only two who needed to retake classes to graduate.

"Hey man," Jeremy said with a nod to his friend.

"Mario Brothers? Sweet! Have you gotten to the seventh world yet?" Michael watched the screen slack-jawed for a while until the character on the screen hopped up to the next platform.

"No, I'm still working on this fourth level of the sixth world," Jeremy said.

After a moment, Michael went to the fridge, grabbed a can of Pepsi, and took a seat in the chair adjacent to the couch, his eyes still glued to the TV. "Try to get that—oh!"

"Two more lives left," Jeremy murmured.

Kathy watched the game for a few more minutes, trying her hardest to get into it, but the excitement from the anticipation of getting to the next level wasn't there for her like it was for the boys.

Instead, she went to the kitchen, pulled the phone from its mount on the wall, and dialed the house. If Jeremy wouldn't talk to her, she could at least check in with her sister and see what she learned about Mark.

"Hello?"

"Sam, hi, it's me."

49

HARPY

"Kathy? What happened to your date?"

She leaned on the tiled counter and stared at the various fruits painted on the tiled backsplash. Jeremy and his friends always said that this house was designed for a woman, not a bunch of college boys. In the end, they were just pictures on a wall. Everything else they needed still worked.

"Eh," she replied. "Uneventful. Jeremy got distracted with his video game and now he and Michael are staring at the screen."

"Are you dating a man or a child?" Samantha asked, then added, "Kidding. Sorry your date didn't turn out that well."

"It's fine. We're just…going through some stuff. We'll work it out."

"I'm sure you will," Samantha said.

"Anyway, what did you find out from Mark?"

"Well, he was reluctant to tell me much. I had to use my power on him."

"Which is why you were the best person to question him," Kathy added.

"Yeah. He claims he doesn't know why the harpies were after him, although I did get out of him that he's been cheating on his wife."

"Can't say I'm surprised, but that hardly seems like something bad enough to kill someone over. Unless you're his wife."

"That's what I was thinking too," Samantha said.

"So we've confirmed that those creatures were harpies who were attacking him?"

"Not officially. I haven't checked the book yet. I just got home."

"Got home from where?" Kathy asked.

"From taking Mark back to his office."

"Sam!" Noting her outburst, Kathy peeked her head around the corner into the living room and saw that the boys were still very consumed by their game. She lowered her voice and muttered, "How could you let him go?"

"I got all I could get out of him. What was I supposed to do? Shackle him in the basement?"

"You could've persuaded him that he is in danger."

"I tried, Kathy, but he wouldn't listen. And he knows we know more than we're letting on. He threatened to take this story to the paper."

Kathy let out a heavy sigh. "He's a real peach, isn't he? So what do we do now?"

"We're going to need to come up with a game plan. First thing's first, though, we need to find out what Mark's hiding."

"How do you suppose we do that if you let him go?" Kathy asked.

"Talk to his wife."

"You know who his wife is?"

"He mentioned her name was Tina," Samantha explained. "I'm sure I'll be able to look them up in the phone book. We

HARPY

could make a house call. After all, we know Mark is still at work."

"For now. If he hasn't already been snatched up and torn apart by those creatures."

"Let's hope that's not the case. In the meantime, we can help him by finding out his secrets. Mark may be a jerk, but he's still a target."

"True," Kathy said. "When do you want to go?"

"As soon as possible. Do you think you could sneak out of your date early?"

Kathy peeked around the corner one more time. "If this is his idea of a date, then he's dating his roommate, not me."

Samantha laughed. "Okay, I'll head out now and come and pick you up."

"Sounds like a plan."

"I just hope we can get some answers before the next attack," Samantha said.

"Me too."

CHAPTER 11

Jeffrey Jackson sat on his couch and watched the grainy television set in the living room with his son curled up next to him. His wife, Sheila, was in the kitchen fixing something nice. The aromas of it wafted into the living room.

Jeffrey put his arm around his son and gave him a sideways hug and a smile. He decided to take a breath and relish in the moment. His life wasn't picture-perfect—he and Sheila had gone through a bad rough patch, to which he was taking full responsibility for—but it was his. It was the life he created. The children he helped create and the woman he promised to adore for the rest of his life.

"Smells good!" he called to his wife.

"You better be hungry!" she shouted back over the loud

exhaust hood over the stove. "There's a lot here!"

Jeffrey patted his belly. "Oh, you know it, baby!"

"It's just about ready."

He turned to his son. "Why don't you go wash your hands before dinner?"

"But they're not dirty!"

Jeffrey gave him a look. "Go wash up." He watched as his son scurried into the kitchen and pulled up a stool to reach the sink.

Leaning back in the couch, Jeffrey thought that he could take a nap right there. But his growling stomach reminded him of just how hungry he was.

"Jeffrey, get in here and help these kids wash up so they can get out of my way!" Sheila called out. "I'm about to trip and drop this pan right on them!"

Using the couch as leverage, Jeffrey rocked once, twice, before he launched his considerable weight off the couch. He made it one step toward the kitchen when the front window crashed in.

"What the hell was that?" Sheila cried out.

He didn't have time to answer her, though. There were three bird-like creatures swarming him, grabbing at him with their talons, sending pain shooting throughout his body. Jeffrey cried out in agony, but the creatures dug their talons in deeper. Together, they lifted him in the air and flew out the window.

CHAPTER 12

Do you have any idea where Glen Crest Drive is?" Kathy asked as her sister drove down East 12th Street back toward the city from Lawrence Park.

"I pulled out a map before I left to double check," Samantha confirmed. "It's off of State Street, near the end."

"Are you sure this is the right couple?"

"There aren't any other Mark and Tina Gads in Erie County. This is as sure as we can be without checking it out."

Kathy nodded. "What's our plan?"

"Well, I guess just be as honest as we can be. Tell her we have reason to believe her husband is in danger because of something he did."

"That's not accusatory *at all*. That'll make his wife go on the defensive!"

"Okay, so maybe we don't say *that*," Samantha said. "Maybe just say we're afraid he might be in danger and try to feel around to see if she'll give up any information that might help us."

"Are we going to play good cop, bad cop?"

"I don't know if that would be the best approach either." Samantha turned onto Parade Street and headed east. "I think we're better off just going as two people who are worried about her husband."

"Worried enough to make a house call? She's going to know we don't really know him."

Samantha sighed. "We'll just have to do our best to get the most information out of her as possible."

Kathy nodded again and watched as they passed through some of the rougher parts of the city. The boarded up factories, houses, and storefronts that spoke to a brighter time in the city's history. It made her sad to see these once-bustling places empty and falling apart.

"So your date wasn't that good, huh?" Samantha asked as she pulled up to the intersection of Parade and East 28th Street.

"It was our typical date, I guess." She shrugged and added, "It was all right."

"But you're looking for more?"

"Just more attention, I guess. I don't know. It's probably just me."

"Kathy, even if it *is* something only you're feeling, you need to be happy in your relationship. If your dates with Jeremy aren't doing it for you anymore, you need to say something." The light turned green and she pulled forward, taking a quick right onto Old French Road.

"It's not that I don't enjoy seeing him," Kathy clarified. "I do! I just want more of his attention." She watched out the window as their surroundings turned more friendly. More suburban. Well-kept yards, freshly-painted houses, clean uncracked sidewalks.

"Well, he's a man and I'm sorry, but he's a little immature too," Samantha said. "So keep that in mind."

"Yeah, yeah. It would be nice to have a deeper conversation with him than where we want to go, who's dating who, or what level he got to on whatever game he's playing."

"Again I'll say, that's who he is." She came to the next intersection and waited at the light. "Not to cut this conversation short, but we're almost there. Think of a good way to start off with Tina."

"You mean you don't have an idea?"

"You shot mine down!"

Kathy let out a deep breath. "I'll think of something."

As the light turned green and Samantha continued straight on, she reached over and grabbed Kathy's hand.

"Hey, everything will be fine. I'm sure you and Jeremy will work it out. And if you don't? It's not the end of the world. You need to worry about *you*, first and foremost."

Kathy squeezed her sister's hand before letting go. "Thanks. I'll have to talk to him just as soon as we make sure this asshole is safe."

Samantha laughed. "Aren't we lucky?"

The Gads lived on a dead-end street among a tangle of other similar streets. There were large mature trees among the slopes of the hill, perfectly manicured houses with privacy from each other and the few passing cars. To top it off, the traffic noise was minimal.

Samantha parked on the street and engaged her parking brake, just in case. The Gad house was a brick ranch at the bottom of a slight hill from the street. Perfect landscaping lined the house and the corner where the concrete driveway met the road. The only sign of imperfection were the bits of grass peeking up in a small crack on the road.

Kathy came around the other side of the car and slipped her hands in her pockets. "So? Are we ready?"

Samantha nodded. "Let's go. Mark might not like the idea of us talking to his wife and if he decides to come home early, we might run into him and we certainly don't want that."

"No, thank you."

The sisters walked down the sloped driveway and followed the sidewalk to the double wooden front doors, which were framed by two brick pillars that each held a large concrete pot of pink wildflowers.

Samantha rang the bell and it took only a minute for a woman in a white sundress to answer the door. Her blonde hair was done in a very stylish wave that carried its own scent of hairspray with it.

"Hello, how can I help you?" she asked in a sweet voice. She pouted her thin lips that were painted with red lipstick, which wasn't even the worst of her makeup tragedies.

"Hi, are you Tina Gad?" Samantha asked.

"Yes, who are you?"

"I'm Samantha and this is my sister Kathy," she said. "Uh, we were wondering if we could come in and talk to you for a minute?"

Tina seemed confused, so Kathy added, "About your husband."

The woman shook her head and started to close the door. "I'm afraid he's not home right now. You'll have to come back later."

Samantha put her hand on the door to stop it from closing. "Yes, we know. That's why we're here now. We're afraid there might be someone who might want to hurt him."

Tina narrowed her eyes and the tone in her voice dropped to something less-than friendly. "Why would you say that?"

"We have a pretty good inclination," Kathy said. "Can we come in and talk?"

"I'm fine talking out here, thanks."

Stifling the urge to roll her eyes, Kathy moved on to her next question. "Do you know of anyone who he might've had a falling out with or someone who may be mad at him for any reason?"

"I don't appreciate your questions prying into our lives," Tina said firmly.

"Mrs. Gad—" Samantha started before she was cut off.

"*Ms.* Gad," she corrected.

"Are you two getting divorced?" Samantha asked plainly.

Tina looked outraged.

"I'm only saying that because when I talked to your husband earlier, he admitted that he's been having an affair."

Kathy was surprised that Samantha seemed to be provoking Tina, but she didn't raise any objections, only listened. Samantha likely had a plan.

"I am not about to spread some gossip with a couple of…*tramps*," Tina spat. "The problems going on with me and my husband are going on between me and my husband."

"Yes, of course," Samantha said. "But he brought in another woman, which really means this involves more people than just the two of you. And the fact that his life is being threatened means that someone is angry enough to want him dead. This affair seems like the best possible reason that we know of."

"For your information, that *girl* is no longer in the picture." Venom fueled Tina's words. "Even if her parents keep trying to remind us with their lawsuit. It's bad enough that we're going to have to face this humiliation in court soon."

"Lawsuit?" Kathy asked. "They're suing you guys?"

Tina ran her tongue over her teeth and studied the sisters. "They're claiming Mark pushed her to suicide."

Samantha and Kathy exchanged looks with each other. Pushing someone to suicide seemed like a good reason for his attack. Both sisters felt a newfound disgust for the man.

"And I don't understand what you two busybodies have to do with any of this," Tina went on. "Leave me and my husband alone! If someone wants him dead, that'll save me the effort of having to divorce him! Now, get off my property before I have to call the police."

"Ma'am, if you could just give us the name of the girl he was seeing," Samantha said, but the door slammed in response. Her shoulders slumped and she turned back to head toward the driveway. "It was worth a shot."

"We need to find out who that girl was," Kathy said. "He was sleeping with her and then she killed herself over it? Sounds like a good reason for those creatures to want him dead. I could think of a few nasty spells to put on him myself."

"You know we can't do that," Samantha said. "As much as we both want to."

"I know, but it would feel good."

Samantha got behind the wheel and buckled up. "I want to head down to Mark's office right now. Catch him before he has a chance to talk to his wife. Maybe I can persuade him to tell us the girl's name."

HARPY

"Your persuasion didn't seem to work on *Ms.* Gad."

"Wasn't using it." Samantha hooked around the cul-de-sac and turned left onto State Street to take them back downtown. "I wanted to see her emotions. See if she wanted him dead or if he had wronged her in any sort of significant way."

"Well that paid off," Kathy said. "I knew you were working on something. Too bad we couldn't get more out of her."

"I think we got enough, though," Samantha said. "We confirmed that he was having an affair and it's a really good possibility that this girl's suicide is the reason there's a target on his back. Now we just need to find out who this girl was and exactly what happened between them."

"Yeah." Kathy was battling her own demons about helping this man who had caused a girl to end her life. Was it the right thing to stop a creature from killing him, even if there were valid reasons for doing so?

Looking out the window, watching as the city turned denser the closer they got to downtown, she tried to put it out of her mind. They didn't know the full story yet, so it was best not to jump to conclusions until they had all the answers. But those answers were not likely to be good ones.

"Whoa! Look over there!" Samantha pointed through the windshield toward the sky. Her eyes flickered back and forth between there and the road.

Kathy looked and saw three birds flying through the air, one leading the other two. "Are those birds or are those—"

"Those are definitely *not* birds," Samantha said. "They're too long to be birds. Those must be the harpies."

"But isn't Mark's office down State Street?" Kathy pointed in front of them.

Samantha signaled and turned down East 18th Street to follow them. "Yeah, but we don't know that he's still there. Maybe he figured out why they're after him and is going to track down that girl's parents."

"Or maybe the harpies found a new target."

"Let's hope that's not the case." Now that they were closer, they could better make out the shape of the harpies. "That's definitely them." Samantha cruised down 18th until the harpies changed course and dropped down toward the earth.

Hooking a quick left onto Wallace Street, which was a tiny alley of a street in an old industrial area right next to the Erie County Prison, Samantha sped up to find the scene of the attack.

Bouncing over potholes, Kathy turned off the radio and listened intently out the open window for any sign of a struggle. Just as Samantha turned left onto East 17th Street, the sounds of screams echoed out along the street.

Throwing the car in park at the end of the street, the sisters got out and raced toward a dilapidated blue house across from a collision shop.

Both sisters stopped short when the three creatures burst through the three front windows, shattering glass all over the

HARPY

small front yard and onto the cracked street. Along with them, they dragged the body of a large man. He screamed for help as they carried him higher and higher into the air, their claws digging deep into his flesh.

"Freeze them!" Samantha yelled to her sister.

Kathy raised her hands, but they were already too far out of range for her magic.

Seconds later, a large woman came out screaming and sobbing, staring up at the sky. "Jeffrey! JEFFREY!"

Realizing it was too late, the woman went weak in the knees and collapsed onto the cracked sidewalk, her shoulders shaking with each sob.

CHAPTER 13

Blue lights swirled, reflecting off the windshield of Samantha's car. The sisters leaned against the hood, watching as the police bustled in and out of the house.

The woman, Sheila Jackson, was ushered back into the house for questioning once police arrived and realized they had an audience. One that consisted of Samantha, Kathy, and a few workers from the collision shop across the street.

Everyone was questioned and the sisters were grateful that they could answer honestly that they didn't know why the man was attacked or what happened specifically. At least that kept any potential problems between them and the law at bay. Now all they needed to do was figure out why Jeffrey Jackson was taken.

HARPY

"That was horrible," Kathy murmured to her sister.

"Not here," Samantha said quietly, watching as another car drove up from the other end of the street. A slick black sedan that appeared to carry the driver and one passenger. "We'll talk in the car."

Kathy nodded and the sisters watched as the car came to a stop on the narrow street. A thin man exited the driver's side and another man—a little pudgier than the first—stepped out of the passenger side with a camera around his neck and immediately started snapping pictures.

It wasn't clear exactly what he was trying to capture. He took shots of the empty street, the three run-down houses, the collision shop, the police cars parked out front. His motto must've been to take as many as he could and throw out the ones he didn't need later.

While the photographer was snapping photos, the thin man ran right up to the first police officer he saw and started throwing out questions.

"What's going on? Was this really an abduction? Is the wife available for comment? Do you have any suspects yet? What is the police department's next step forward in bringing this man home?"

"Alan, I need you to step back," one of the officers standing just outside the door to the Jackson house said. "You'll get your interviews in just as soon as we finish ours."

"Do you have any—"

The front door opened and both sisters took a step forward as Sheila Jackson walked out with an older policeman as her escort. Two small boys around the age of ten followed behind her and Samantha felt her heart break a little more for what the family was going through.

Feeling brave, Kathy took several feet closer to the front door, careful to leave enough room for the family to get to the waiting police car without issue.

Alan and his photographer, however, didn't offer the Jacksons the privilege of privacy.

"Ma'am! What happened here? Do you have anything to say? Any message you want to let the public know?"

The woman shook her head, keeping it low, and ushered her kids toward the police car.

"Did your husband have any enemies? Did anyone have any reason to take him hostage?"

Now we're getting somewhere with these questions, Kathy thought to herself.

Once her children were safely in the back of the police car, Sheila turned to Alan, his photographer snapping several pictures of her tear-streaked face.

"Listen closely, because this is all I'll have to say on the matter." She wiped her eyes with a balled up tissue and breathed in a shuddering breath. "My husband is not perfect. He's lied and he's cheated, but he's always come home. He's always provided for us." Her voice was shaky and she sniffled. "And he's always loved us. Yes, he's made mistakes, but he's a good man. He's a good father. And he's my husband. Now I just hope that we're able to find him and bring him home to us, where he belongs, so we can provide for him in the same way he's always provided for us."

"Ma'am, do you have any indication on where he might've been taken? Or who might've taken him?"

Sheila shook her head and turned to get in the car next to her children. "That is all I have to say. Please respect my family's privacy."

The police officer closed the back door for her, got in the front, and drove off toward Parade Street.

Shortly after the Jackson family pulled away, the reporter tried to get more quotes from the responding officers, but didn't get much else, other than the canned response that the department would release a statement once they knew more.

"So?" Kathy asked when she returned to her sister.

Samantha nodded to the car and they both got in. She started the engine, backed up slowly onto Wallace Street, and headed for home.

"That was…" Kathy started.

"I know. Bad."

"But why him? Wouldn't those creatures just want to go after Mark again and again until they finally get him?"

"Maybe they're trying to send us a message that if we keep protecting Mark, they'll take someone else."

"But Jeffrey Jackson? The way his wife was crying for him, I can't imagine he's done anything terrible. At least not as bad as Mark Gad, otherwise he would've been the first target."

"People can surprise you," Samantha said. "Maybe he had secrets his wife didn't know about."

"That's a big maybe."

"But let's look at the facts. *He* was the one who was taken away, not anyone else. He must've done something bad."

"His wife said he's lied and he's cheated," Kathy said. "Maybe she meant that he's cheated on her."

"But does that justify him being attacked like that?"

"Not to me, it doesn't. I just wish we could've stopped it."

"Me too," Samantha said.

They were quiet until Samantha turned onto Cherry Street. The sun was starting to fade, but the day's heat was still present. Kathy rested her arm on the edge of the open window and felt the breeze hit her face. She tried to let the peacefulness of the weather calm her down, but all she kept thinking about was watching as Jeffrey Jackson was carried away and the sounds of his wife screaming for him.

Turning back inside the stuffy car, she said to Samantha, "When we get home, I'm going to get a positive ID on what exactly those creatures are."

"Good idea. Maybe then we can figure out what they want and how to get rid of them. If it's a potion or a spell or something, maybe we can even whip one up tonight and take care of them before they hurt anyone else."

"I just wish I understood the connection between Mark and Jeffrey," Kathy went on. "Did Jeffrey lead some girl to kill herself too?"

"If his wife said he cheated, maybe he cheated on her with the same girl Mark was having an affair with."

"That seems highly unlikely. Mark lives in a nice, perfectly landscaped house on the edge of the city and Jeffrey lived on a side street with cracked pavement right by the prison. They're from two totally different social circles. I doubt they knew any of the same people."

Samantha shrugged and turned left onto their street. "I'm just shooting out ideas here. We'll know more once we check the book."

She pulled into the driveway and stopped short. A red pickup truck was parked in Samantha's usual spot. Steven's truck.

"What's he doing here?" Kathy asked. "Did you guys have a date?"

Samantha turned off the car and stared at her boyfriend's truck for a moment. "Uh...I don't think so. It's been a long day, so I can't even remember."

They got out and walked inside. The scents of a home-cooked meal greeted them as they stepped through the door. A fresh vase of flowers sat in the middle of the dining room table where there were two plate settings and two glasses of wine.

"Steven?" Samantha called.

"Oh, there you are." He emerged from the kitchen with a stained white apron tied around his waist. He wore jeans and a black button-down shirt. "I was wondering when you'd be home." He noticed the look on her face and briefly looked at Kathy before turning back to Samantha. "You didn't remember I was making you dinner tonight, did you?"

She made a face. "I'm sorry! It's just, I had the interview this morning, then I went to lunch with Kathy, and…well, it's been a long day."

"Oh." He looked back at the table, then turned to face her, unsure of what to do.

"But this is a nice surprise to come home to." She stepped forward and kissed him. "Thank you, sweetheart. I love it and I'm sure it's delicious."

Steven looked over Samantha's shoulder to Kathy. "Well, I thought it'd just be the two of us and I'm not sure there's enough—"

Kathy put up her hands. "Don't worry about me! I'll just make a quick sandwich and then head upstairs and leave you two alone. You won't even know I'm here." She brushed past them and escaped into the kitchen.

"You told me your sister would be out with Jeremy tonight," he murmured to Samantha after Kathy had left the room.

She sighed, finally remembering the conversation they had earlier in the week when they planned this date. "I know, I'm

HARPY

sorry. I completely blanked with everything."

"Well, couldn't you suggest she go see him now?"

"I can't do that," she whispered. "They had a date earlier today and...they're having a little issue. Nothing crazy, but I think she needs time away from Jeremy to think about things."

"But what about us?" Steven asked.

"She said she'd be upstairs. We'll have our date. Don't worry about her. She'll keep her distance."

He pulled her in for a hug, just as Kathy emerged from the kitchen with a sandwich wrapped in a paper towel.

"Oh! Sorry! This is the last you'll see of me! Promise!" She started up the stairs, but Samantha called to her.

"Are you going to check the, uh—"

"I'm on it!" Kathy said. "And I'll work on anything else that needs to be done for it."

"Thank you!"

When Kathy disappeared up the stairs, Steven looked down at Samantha with a confused look.

"Shopping list," Samantha lied quickly. "She's checking the, uh, number of *lady items* we have."

Steven's eyebrows shot up. "Oh. Never mind then. Shall we eat? And talk about something else entirely?"

Samantha laughed. "Yes, that sounds great to me."

CHAPTER 14

- NOVEMBER 1953 -

Sharon was starting to break a sweat as she bustled around the kitchen to prepare what she hoped to be a delicious Thanksgiving dinner. It was the first time she had prepared it on her own, but she had her Betty Crocker cookbook to guide her through it.

"Smells good, honey," Patrick called from the living room in between shouts to the radio as the football game was announced. "I like what I see!"

Smiling, Sharon checked the turkey in the oven. She couldn't quite make out what the thermometer said, but the book said it would take three hours in the oven and it wasn't quite time yet. Instead, she turned to the pot on the stove and mashed the potatoes.

HARPY

She moved on to set the table, making sure there were no visible pots and pans in the dining area since Patrick hated to look at a mess when he ate. By time she finished laying out the silverware, the timer rang to note that the turkey was done.

"Turn that down!" Patrick barked from the living room.

Sharon lifted the tray holding the turkey onto the cooktop and checked the thermometer. Several degrees over 165. Ready to be sliced.

"Sweetheart, did you want to carve the turkey?"

Patrick waved her off and leaned forward on the couch, staring at the radio set. He took a swig of his beer and Sharon noted the small collection of bottles he had on the table beside the couch. But, she reasoned with herself, those had been consumed over the course of the whole day.

Turning back to the kitchen, she worked on the turkey, slicing the small bird into servings for her and her husband. She laid the carvings out on a platter that she carried over to the crowded dining room table. It was much too small for the meal she had prepared, but it was what they had.

She pulled off her apron, refreshed her glass of water, and stepped into the living room. With her hands behind her back, she proudly said, "Dinner is ready. Turn off the radio and come eat."

For a brief moment, she felt a flicker of fear run through her as she realized she had doled out orders to her husband. He hated being told what to do, especially by her. But to her

74

surprise, he got off the couch, turned off the radio, and came to the table.

"This looks delicious, dear," he said. "Hope it tastes half as good as it smells."

Sharon sat across from him and folded her napkin in her lap. "Go easy on me, it was my first time making it." She watched in anticipation as Patrick dished out his food.

In her heart she wished they could spend the holiday with more people. Since moving to Washington, they didn't have any family in the area. And Patrick's friends were all from the garage, who had wives and families of their own to celebrate with. Sharon herself didn't have very many friends because Patrick liked to keep close tabs on her to make sure she was working to create a good home for the two of them.

Sharon dished out her own plate, noting how quiet it was. Over most dinners, Patrick usually told her about his day. Since he had the day off, they didn't have anything to talk about. Only the sound of clinking silverware on the china they got for their wedding filled the room.

Patrick cut into his turkey and took a bite.

"So what do you think?" she asked, watching him as he chewed.

"It's dry."

She frowned and reached for the gravy. "Here, add this."

He ignored her offering and took another bite. "Potatoes are cold, too."

Harpy

"I'm sorry," she muttered. "It was only me in the kitchen and I had so many things going at once that it was hard to make sure everything came out hot—"

"It tastes horrible." He spit out his mouthful on the plate.

Sharon laughed nervously and rose to her feet. "Don't be crass, dear. Here, I'll fix you another plate."

"I'm not eating it."

She looked at him from the kitchen, where she was reaching for another clean dish. "Don't be silly. We have this whole turkey to eat." She walked back over to the table and started preparing a second helping for Patrick.

"How much did you pay for this turkey?" he asked.

"Well, it was the holiday, so it was a *bit* more—"

He grabbed her wrist and she stopped fussing with the food.

"How much?"

She told him.

"And you went and pissed it all down the drain when you burnt it to a crisp!" he shouted, finally releasing her.

"It's not burnt—"

"You ruined this turkey, Sharon, and wasted *my* money. Money I worked hard for. Now you expect me to eat this garbage?"

She studied him. Knew that the beers he had been drinking all day were partly responsible for his behavior. He didn't act this nasty when he wasn't drinking. But she had spent all day in the kitchen and she wasn't going to let him throw a tantrum and ruin her day's work.

"I wouldn't call it garbage, dear," she said as softly as she could. It was all she could do to stifle the fear and anger bubbling inside her.

"Then you eat it."

"I can't eat this whole turkey by—" A hot piece of turkey hit her cheek and stuck to her for a second from the gravy. A moment later, it fell to the floor.

"Eat it, Sharon. Don't waste my money!"

She wiped the gravy from her cheek with a napkin. "Honey, there is nothing wrong with—"

He threw another piece of turkey at her. Then a handful of potatoes.

Contrary to what he said, the potatoes *were* hot and she felt her skin ache from the heat. Quickly, she wiped it away. "Don't act like a child!"

Before she realized what she'd said, she could see his lips curling in anger as he shot up to his feet, grabbed his plate, and spilled the remaining contents all over her.

She cried out and sunk to the floor. The food burned her skin and she wondered if he was going to hit her again. The warm gravy dripped all over her, clinging to the dress she had so carefully ironed the night before for what was supposed to be a special occasion.

Patrick reached for the gravy boat and before he could confirm her suspicions, she held up her hand and a magical gust of wind sent him flying back into the living room. The gravy boat smashed against the wall, splattering gravy all over.

Sharon barely had time to get to her feet before he came rushing at her, driving his fist into her gut—careful not to leave a mark like he did last time.

"If you *ever* use your magic on me again, I'm going to *kill* you!" he shouted at her, even though she was only inches away from him. Spittle flew from his mouth and landed on her as he shouted, adding insult to injury. "Do you understand me?"

She nodded.

"Answer me, Sharon." He grabbed her sticky chin and forced her to look at him. "Speak."

She gulped down her fear and nodded again. "I understand."

He walked off into the kitchen and grabbed an apple from the fridge before retreating to the living room. "Clean up this mess."

Feeling humiliated and defeated, with shaky hands Sharon began picking up the dinner she had spent all day cooking. While she worked, she did he best to stifle her tears.

CHAPTER 15

I must say, it's nice to finally get you alone." Steven reached across the table and held Samantha's hand.

He had laid out a red tablecloth, free from wrinkles. Several candles surrounded the room, giving it a warm orange glow and a pleasant fruity aroma. Their meal lay before them, covered by a pot lid to keep it warm. It was the only flaw in elegance on the table, but Samantha overlooked that.

She smiled and rolled her eyes. "We just had a fancy date last week."

"Which was cut short because…"

Samantha thought about it and then remembered. "Right. Kathy needed a ride—but we got through dinner just the two of us! And we had a good talk in the car. *And* I suggested we go

HARPY

back to your place after we dropped her off…"

Steven put up his hands in defense. "I don't want to fight. I just wish we could spend time together without the presence of your sister."

"She's not here now."

"She's upstairs."

"But it's not like she's listening!"

He smiled. "I get it that you're close to your sister. As a matter of fact, I admire the relationship you two have. But there are times when I'd prefer it be just the two of us."

Samantha nodded. "I hear where you're coming from and I see your point, but at the same time, Kathy and I live together. She doesn't have a car. This is what I'm bringing to the table. I'll do my best to make sure the two of us have alone time, but there's only so much I can do. You need to meet me halfway."

He smiled at her. "Are you sure you want to be an accountant and not a counselor?"

Her eyebrows jumped up as she reached for her glass of wine on the table. "Trust me, I would rather rely on the certainty of numbers than the uncertainty of emotions."

"I can't argue with that." He reached for the pot lid and lifted it, followed by a waft of steam rising through the candlelit air. "We should eat before this cools off completely."

She handed him her bowl and her dished her out a heaping helping of coconut shrimp fried rice.

"Oh wow, this looks delicious." She took her bowl back and

set it in front of her. "I didn't realize you could do all of this."

"Well, one of your cookbooks helped," he added with a chuckle. He set his full bowl down and covered what remained in the pot.

Samantha scooped up her first bite and blew on it before trying it.

"What do you think?" Steven asked, his wine glass raised to his mouth.

She made funny noises as she tried to taste the food without completely burning her tongue. She failed and swallowed it down quickly. "It's good. Hot."

He cringed. "Sorry. I thought it sat long enough to cool."

She gulped down half her glass of water—he had thought of everything. "No, I'm sure once the skin grows back on my tongue I'll love it."

They laughed.

"I'll hold off on mine for a minute, then," he said. "But otherwise it's good?"

She scooped up her next bite and took longer to blow on it. She nodded. "Very good. Thank you for making it."

"Of course," he said. "I'd do anything for you."

"Easy now," she warned. "Don't get caught up in the moment and promise something you can't deliver on."

He smiled. "All right, then. Let the record show that I make no promises to make dinner for you in the future. Let each time I do it be a surprise."

She laughed. "Wait a minute, I screwed that up somehow."

Steven held up his hands. "Hey, the deal's been done."

She put up a finger as the events of that morning came back to her. "Speaking of deals, I had another interview this morning with Darius Wilcox." Had it really only been that morning? It'd been a long day.

"Oh yeah?" Steven's face lit up. "How'd that go?"

"Really well, actually." His smile was contagious because now she was beaming just as much as he was. "He seemed impressed by the internships I've done and I guess my recommendations said some good things about me too."

"I'm sure they said *terrific* things about you," Steven corrected.

She felt her face flush and was grateful for the dim lighting. "Yeah, well, Mr. Marsden, who I interviewed with, said I'd be moving on to the next round—which is the final round."

"Samantha, that's great!" Steven cheered. "Congratulations!"

"I need to remember to send him a thank you card..."

Steven smirked and asked, "Who's the next round with?"

She made a face. "It's in front of a panel."

"Any idea who's on it?"

"No, he said he still needed to put it together."

"That's if he even does."

"Why would you say that?"

"He might just call you up and offer you the job."

She gave him a disbelieving look. "They still need to go

through the formalities."

"Not necessarily."

"And I'm sure they have other candidates they're considering just as much as me."

"Sam, I very much doubt that," he said. "You love what you do, you're meticulous, and you're very well organized." He would know, being an accountant himself as well. "Who else would send a thank you card after each interview?"

"Someone who wants a job!"

"Not everyone," he said. "If you ask me, this thing is yours."

Samantha took a deep breath and reached for her wine glass again. "I don't know if I'd go *that* far. It hasn't even been twelve hours since we met."

"I'm sure he knew as soon as you walked in the door."

She dug back into her food. "Anyway, how was your day?"

He reached across the table and squeezed her hand. "I'm so proud of you."

She returned his smile. "Thank you. I just don't want to jinx anything by making assumptions before anything's official."

"All right, all right, I get it. I'll back off." He poked around his helping of his dinner. "How was my day? Uh…not bad. Kind of quiet. Worked on a few reports for a few different clients. I had to call—"

Heavy footsteps bounding down the stairs cut him off. He shot Samantha a look across the table that asked, *I thought she wouldn't bother us?*

HARPY

Desperately, Samantha pleaded back with her own look. *Sorry! What do you want me to do?*

"Sam!" Kathy called, then stopped when she noted the candles and the food and the wine. "Oh, this looks so romantic! What is that? Fried rice and...chicken?" She leaned over to try to get a glimpse of Steven's bowl. "Oh, no, that's shrimp. Couldn't tell in this light."

"Kathy, what do you want?" Samantha asked briskly.

"Oh, sorry. I don't want to interrupt. I just...um..." She swallowed hard and looked between her sister and Steven, regretting crashing their evening. But what she had to say couldn't wait—no matter the repercussions. "I need to talk to you."

"Now?"

Kathy cringed, knowing exactly the harm she was causing. "If I could."

Samantha looked to Steven, who sighed and rose to his feet.

"No, don't get up," she pleaded. "I'll be right back."

He collected their dishes. "No, go on. We can heat these up later."

"Steven..." she called to him, but didn't know what else to say. When he had disappeared into the kitchen, she got up and led Kathy over to the dark living room to have a private conversation.

She knew Kathy wouldn't have interrupted their date if it wasn't important.

84

CHAPTER 16

I'm so sorry," Kathy whispered, reaching for Samantha's hands. Her sister pushed her away and crossed her arms. "It's fine. What did you find?"

Kathy looked between her sister and the doorway to the kitchen on the other side of the house and let out a heavy sigh. She hated that she just crashed Samantha's date. Again. But Samantha's dates always seemed to occur at the worst times: when some magical nuisance needed attending.

"Well, first off, I checked the book and as far as I could tell, those bird creatures *are* harpies."

"Which is what we figured," Samantha said. "What do they want?"

"According to the entry, they're also known as 'seizers' or

'snatchers,' probably because they're typically able to pluck their targets up and carry them off."

"Like they did with Jeffrey Jackson."

"Yes. Well, unless their targets run, like Mark Gad."

Samantha nodded. "True. How do they choose their targets? Where do they take them? How do we get rid of them?"

Kathy clenched her jaw. "Um…bad news or good news first?"

The older sister sighed and glanced back toward the kitchen for any sign of Steven. Nothing. "Kathy, just give me everything. I don't have time for this."

"I think we need to make time."

Samantha dropped her arms and let out an angry breath.

"Only because Mark Gad could still be in danger," Kathy added quickly.

"Yes, because he's such a gem."

Kathy gave her sister a look. "I'm with you, Mark Gad is a jerk, who could very likely have pushed a girl to kill herself. I don't want to save him either. But that's not up to us. We need to make a good faith effort to protect him. At least until we know the whole story and for right now, he's a potential victim."

Samantha put a hand on her hip and rubbed her eyes with her free hand. "I know. I'm just…frustrated."

"I get it. Did you want me to go after him alone?"

"No," she said quickly. "It's too dangerous. Is there anything else? Why are the harpies after him?"

"We obviously haven't confirmed the specifics of Mark's story yet, but the book says that harpies go after people who commit horrible sins and snatch them up and carry them off to the underworld to pay for those sins."

"Horrible sins like sleeping with a girl and then pushing her to suicide?"

Kathy nodded. "Right, but again, we need to confirm that's what happened before we make judgements about Mark. Maybe there's another explanation."

"I doubt it."

"Me too, but there's more."

"*More?*" Samantha looked back to the dining room and briefly caught Steven's eye as he finished clearing the table.

"Side note, which is kind of random: harpies are drawn away by the sound of a brass instrument."

"Too bad neither one of us plays the tuba."

"No, but there might be something like that in the attic.," Kathy said.

"And you couldn't have looked for that before you crashed my date?"

Kathy's brow scrunched. "I'm sorry!"

"It's fine. Go on."

Again, Kathy studied her sister for a moment before continuing, "Well, I was thinking that it didn't make sense that the harpies went after Jeffrey Jackson when Mark Gad was still running around free."

87

HARPY

"Maybe Jeffrey did something equally horrible too."

"But it didn't sound like Jeffrey had done anything as bad as Mark," the younger witch countered. "Granted, we haven't really done any kind of investigating into him, but from what his wife said, Jeffrey was a good person, even if he had a tendency to lie and cheat."

"Yes, because lying and cheating are two virtues of a good person."

"We don't know how bad the lies were or what exactly he cheated on."

"My guess is he cheated on his wife."

"Right, but Mrs. Jackson also said that her husband always took care of the family and always came home."

Samantha glanced back at the kitchen doorway again. She could hear the sound of running water. Steven was probably doing the dishes. Her heart panged at the thought. "People in relationships don't know everything about the other. Secrets still exist."

Kathy knew her sister was talking about the ultimate secret they both needed to keep from the men in their lives: that they were witches. Lying to the people they were trying to get close to hurt them again and again. Tonight just happened to be another one of those moments for Samantha.

"Sam, if you don't want to do this—"

"So what's your point about the harpies? Did they come to Erie with a list of horrible men to pick up or is their true target Mark?"

88

"I think they're here for Mark, but because we stopped them from taking him, they're viewing him as protected. I think that's why they're going after people like Jeffrey."

"People who haven't committed sins as bad as Mark because they can't get what they really want."

"Exactly. So unless they get who they came for, I don't think these harpies are going away," Kathy explained. "As much as we both agree that Mark is a horrible person who's probably done bad things, we can't just sacrifice him to save other people. That's not our job. We need to try to protect as many people as possible."

"Which means we need to find Mark as soon as possible," Samantha said with a sigh.

"Yeah," Kathy said quietly. "And we need to come up with a way to stop the harpies."

"The book didn't have anything?"

Kathy shook her head. "Not that I could find."

"Okay. Why don't you try to come up with something and I'll go tell Steven the bad news."

"Sam, I'm really sorry about all of this."

"It's not your fault." She squeezed her sister's hand. "You made the right call. We need to find him and make sure he's safe."

Turning, Samantha stepped toward the kitchen, thinking of a good excuse to tell Steven along the way. No matter how slow she walked, it still wasn't enough time to come up with anything good. There was nothing good about this situation. She wanted to spend the evening with her boyfriend, but she couldn't. Worse, she couldn't even explain why she had to leave. This was not the making of a healthy relationship.

When she stepped into the kitchen, Steven was drying his hands at the sink. A stack of clean dishes sat on another dish towel on the counter.

"Thanks for cleaning up." She forced a smile, but his cold expression wiped it away.

"Is everything okay?"

Samantha swallowed hard. "Um…not really. I…have to run out. With Kathy."

He huffed and shook his head. "Figures."

"Please don't be like that."

"How do you expect me to be?" He tossed the towel on the island table. "We made plans for tonight, Samantha! Just the two of us! Apparently, I'm the only one who remembered that. Or cared."

"I care!" She took a step toward him, but the daggers he shot at her with his eyes prevented her from completely closing the gap. Instead, she stayed safely on the other side of the island. "Steven, there's nothing more I'd rather do than stay here and continue our date. But I can't."

"Why not?"

She dropped her eyes down. "You just have to trust me."

"Oh my G—you seriously aren't going to tell me?"

"I wish I could!" she roared back. "Believe me, there's nothing more I'd rather do than to lay it all out there for you. But I can't. And you just need to trust me on that. Please."

His chest heaved as he studied her. "Samantha, you know I love you, but you make it so damn hard to have a relationship with you. Are you sure you even want to be with me?"

"Of course I do! I love you too."

"Then we need to change the way we do things." He stepped to the door and grabbed his keys from the hook. "We need to actually see each other in order to have a real relationship. If you can't commit to that, then maybe we need to rethink some things."

"No, Steven, please—" She stopped herself. Please what? What did she expect him to do? Stay? That wasn't an option. She needed to go with Kathy to protect an asshole from paying for the sin of ruining a girl's life. None of this felt right to her, and yet she knew it was.

He let out a deep breath and said in a calmer voice, "We both need to think about things. Call me when you're ready to talk."

CHAPTER 17

Mark Gad burst through the door from the garage and stepped first into the kitchen, then the den on a hunt for his wife. With his heart racing, he finally found her out on the desk in the back, laying in a lounge chair with a martini and smoking a cigarette.

Odd. Tina didn't smoke. Not anymore.

"Tina! Get inside!" He looked up at the sky nervously.

She jumped, nearly spilling some of her drink all over herself. "Holy shit, Mark. You scared the living daylights out of me!"

He waved into the house. "Inside! Come on! Hurry!"

"What the hell is this about?" She threw her feet onto the deck, but didn't get up. Instead, she puffed her cigarette. She was wrapped in a pink housecoat, yet still had her makeup on, lest any neighbors see her without it.

Mark stepped toward her and pulled the cigarette away from her and flicked it in the yard. "What's this? You don't smoke!"

"Don't yell at me," she countered. "I've had a long day. Is there something you want to tell me, my dear, *loving* husband?" She rolled her eyes and long took a sip of her drink.

"I'll explain inside, hurry up! Before they come!"

Tina got to her feet and stepped toward him, wobbling only slightly. Clearly, not on her first drink. "Who, Mark? Those whores who came to the house earlier? Are you having another affair? They were asking about the other girl you were sleeping with."

"No, Tina, that's done—I'm not—those girls—" He stopped and looked up at the sky again, stepping further out onto the deck to look onto the roof. His eyes quickly scanned the neighboring houses as well. "You know what, never mind. Just get inside and I'll tell you everything."

"What are you looking for?" she asked. "Afraid someone set cameras up? Is that why you're so insistent on getting me into the house? You think the neighbors will hear about your little call girls on the side and embarrass you? Well welcome to my world, Mark! I've had to endure humiliation at your hands for our entire marriage and I'm tired of it!"

Out in the distance, he saw the three bird-women approach.

HARPY

They perched themselves on the neighbor's fence behind them and watched. His wife was too intoxicated to notice.

"Please, Tina, let's go inside! Now! I'm only worried about you."

She scoffed and took another sip of her martini and waved the glass around, spilling some of the contents. "If that were true, you wouldn't have stepped out of our marriage. You know why I stole one of your precious pack of cigarettes, Mark? It's because I needed to relax and I was all out of those special little pills you had a doctor prescribe me!"

Finally, Mark grabbed Tina by the wrist and pulled her into the house, slamming the sliding door and locking it behind her. Once they were inside, he closed the blinds over the sliding door and rushed through the rest of the house to do the same.

"You don't get to touch me like that, Mark!" Tina shouted at him as he moved through the house. "You don't get to touch me at all!" She went to take another sip of her drink, but realized it was empty and tossed the glass on a nearby recliner.

Mark, who was only half listening to his wife, came back into the room and asked, "Where are the kids?"

"They're at a friends house," she said, studying her manicured nails. "Mommy needed a mental health evening, which you went and ruined."

"Tina, listen to me, we might be in danger."

She stumbled to the couch and laid down. The effects of the alcohol suddenly hitting her. "No, you're in danger." She

94

yawned. "In danger from that lawsuit. In danger of losing your money, this house, your kids. Not to mention me, but you don't seem to care about that. Don't be surprised if you see divorce papers coming soon."

"We can talk about that later," he said. "First, I need you to listen to me. I was attacked today—and then forced to go with these girls who have these *powers* or something. I don't know. They—Tina?"

His wife was no longer listening. Sprawled out on the couch, Tina Gad had fallen asleep, completely oblivious that her husband was trying to have a conversation with her.

Frustrated, Mark went to the window and pulled back the blinds, only slightly, to peek outside. The creatures—or those women—were still perched on the fence in the back, staring into the house. He only hoped they wouldn't come after him and his wife—or his kids—while they slept. They deserved a little reprieve.

At least, he hoped they did.

CHAPTER 18

"What if the door's locked?" Kathy asked as the witches walked up to Mark's office building downtown. They had parked the car in a nearby parking garage.

It was the first time that either one of them had spoken since they left the house. The car ride was tense. Kathy could tell Samantha was upset but didn't want to ask if she was okay for fear that her sister's anger would be diverted to her.

Besides, how could Samantha be okay? She was powerless to the things happening in her life and one thing that Samantha hated more than anything was to not have control.

"We'll have to make sure to check all the entrances," Samantha said. "Let's start with the back. There'll be a smaller chance of being caught on camera."

Kathy hadn't thought of that. She immediately changed her direction away from the sidewalk to the small alley between the parking garage on French and East 10th to stay in stride with her sister. Samantha was power-walking faster than the old ladies at the mall. The only thing separating the two was that Samantha didn't have that swift arm pumping motion going. And her scowl certainly spoke volumes.

Around the corner, they found a small nondescript service door at the back of the building. Tugging on the handle, Samantha wasn't able to budge it. It was locked.

Slamming her hand against the metal door, she let out an ounce of frustration. "Dammit!"

"Now what?" Kathy asked.

Annoyed, Samantha quickly recited:

Our path is blocked,
So please unlock.

It was one of the simplest spells Samantha had ever recited and she wasn't sure it would even work, but a few seconds later they heard a faint click and when she pulled on the door again, it swung open without resistance.

"Okay then," Kathy muttered as she followed her sister in.

Inside, they walked into a dank stairwell. Samantha immediately started up the noisy metal stairs circling up to the top of the building.

HARPY

"Which floor?" Kathy asked from behind, her voice carrying up through the cavernous space.

Samantha stopped, leaned in close to her sister, and whispered, "Tenth floor. I looked up the insurance company he works for in the yellow pages."

Kathy nodded and followed her sister up the rest of the way.

By time they reached the correct floor, both sisters were sweating from the heat—both outside and from the stuffiness of the stairwell. Despite the late hour, the June warmth didn't relent.

Samantha wiped the sweat off her forehead with her wrist before opening the metal door onto the floor. The exertion was just what she needed to let out some of her frustration.

The sisters walked down a hallway with ornate moulding and cracked terrazzo floors. Signs of a more prestigious time. Rounding the corner, Samantha quickly held out her hand to push her sister back into the hall where they couldn't be seen.

"What?" Kathy whispered softly.

"I wasn't planning on anyone being here other than Mark."

"Who else is here?"

"Cleaning crews."

"Any sign of Mark?"

Samantha shook her head. "I couldn't tell. You think you can sneak up and freeze them?"

"Do I even need to sneak up?" Kathy asked. "By time my

magic wears off, we'll be in and out."

"Just be careful."

Leaving her older sister in the cover of the hallway, Kathy stepped around the corner into the office for Blue Water Insurance. Only half of the fluorescent lights were on, casting eerie shadows thanks to the cubicles. The cleaning cart sat in the middle of the the maze of partition walls and one woman collected and replaced trash bags while another vacuumed the carpet.

Hunkering behind one of the partition walls, Kathy waited until the woman collecting the trash bags bent over to retrieve another one. Putting up her hands, Kathy froze the room in time, both cleaning women stopping what they were doing, oblivious to being under the influence of magic. Even the vacuum stopped running.

Turning back into the hallway, Kathy waved her sister forward.

"Okay, we need to make this quick," Samantha said. "Doesn't look like Mark's here."

"It's late. He must've gone home."

"Which makes sense, but that doesn't mean this needs to be a wasted trip." Samantha moved through the cubicles, moving past the woman who had been frozen by Kathy's magic while collecting trash bags.

"What are you looking for?" Kathy followed hesitantly.

"Mark's desk. His wife mentioned that that girl's parents are suing him. What's the most likely place that he would've gotten served?"

"At the office," Kathy replied, understanding where her sister was heading.

"Right. He may have told his wife about the lawsuit, but that doesn't mean he brought the paperwork home for her to learn all the details of the case." She stopped at one cubicle in the corner. "Ah, here it is."

Kathy stood just outside the cubicle and looked around. First, at the women frozen by her magic, then out the window into the hallway. She didn't want them to be seen by anyone. That would be hard to explain themselves out of.

Oblivious to Kathy's paranoia, Samantha sat in Mark's office chair, flicked on his desk lamp for extra light, and began riffling through his things. Time sheets, pay stubs, and receipts sat in one pile. Small notes scattered around his desk, tucked into the corners of the desk calendar, stashed under the corner of the picture frames that held photos of his wife and kids.

Samantha scanned the dates on the calendar. All seemed to be work-related. Department meeting on the 7th at 10:00. Paydays on the 3rd and 17th. Phone interview with Adamson on the 15th at 3:00.

"How much longer?" Kathy asked. "I don't know how long my magic will hold."

"Relax, you can just freeze them again." Samantha turned her attention to the desk drawers. She was determined to find something helpful for them. Otherwise, she had ruined her date for nothing.

"Yeah, but in that split second, they might see something and get suspicious."

"I'm hurrying, I'm hurrying." Samantha slid open the main drawer and found a collection of pens and pencils, a calculator, a cigarette lighter, and a pile of scrap paper.

Supplies, that was it.

Slamming that shut, she noticed Kathy wincing at the noise out of the corner of her eye. "We'll be fine."

"Let's go," her sister said. "I don't like this."

"Just two more drawers."

Pulling at the top drawer on the side of the desk, Samantha was frustrated that it was locked. Instead, she moved her attention to the bottom drawer, which opened with a loud screech.

File folders hung inside, stuffed with active account files. Samantha guessed that all the other files were in the filing cabinets lined up at the back of the office, where the cleaning woman stood frozen mid-vacuum. Nothing personal to Mark would be in those files. If they were going to find anything, it would be at his desk.

She sifted through the files, focusing on the folders on the ends. Mark would want easy access in case he got a phone call related to the case or if another lawyer decided to make a visit.

As far as Samantha could tell, all the folders contained

account files. Unless he stashed the lawsuit papers in with one of the files. She grabbed the first folder, plopped it on the desk and began sifting through it.

"Now what are you doing?" Kathy asked.

"Looking for anything about the lawsuit. Even if all we get is the name of the victim, we'll be able to look into her. See if you can find a key for that top drawer."

Sighing, Kathy grabbed the coffee cup from the corner of the desk that held a pile of keys and tried to slide each one into the lock for the drawer. None of them seemed to work.

"Nothing in this file," Samantha said, closing the folder and turning to replace it.

"We don't have time to sort through them all," Kathy said. "These women are going to unfreeze at any minute. We need to get out of here."

"Hold on. What's this?" Samantha reached into the gap in the bottom drawer left by the folder she had already retrieved and pulled out a folded court document.

"What is it?"

Slowly, she unfolded it and skimmed through it. "Looks like we found the name of our victim—well, her parents. Unless he's being sued by more than one person. Can't say I'd be surprised about that."

"What are their names?" Kathy leaned over her sister's shoulder to read the summons.

"Robert and Debra Powers."

DAVID NETH

"Look, it's dated last month," Kathy pointed out. "I wonder how long ago that girl killed herself."

"That's all stuff we can find out later," Samantha said. "At least now we have a lead."

"Yeah, let's pack up and get out of here before these women unfreeze and we scare them to death."

Samantha replaced the folder, clicked off the desk lamp, and followed her sister out of the office. Just as they rounded the corner into the hallway leading back to the staircase, they heard the roar of the vacuum again as the cleaning women unfroze.

103

CHAPTER 19

Coffee, *please*," Kathy said groggily as she trudged into the kitchen the next morning. The pitter-patter of her bare feet on the hardwood were yet another sign that she hadn't completely woken up yet.

The phone started ringing again and she whined at the sound. Granted, it was 10:00 in the morning, but she was in a dead sleep until the incessant ringing again and again forced her out of bed.

"That's probably Jeremy." Samantha was in the kitchen in her bathrobe with her hair up. "He called a few times this morning already." She pulled the carafe out and poured a cup for Kathy.

"Let it ring." Kathy took a seat at the island and cradled her coffee. "I'm not ready to talk to him."

Samantha poured Cheerios into a bowl. "He's only going to keep calling."

"He'll get the hint eventually." Kathy took a sip of her coffee and felt the warmth run through her body. Not that she needed to warm up. The morning sun shining through the kitchen window was already heating up the room, forecast to be another scorcher.

Blessedly, the phone stopped ringing and Kathy asked, "Are you just getting up? This is the latest you've slept in a long time."

"We had a long night." Samantha pulled the milk out of the fridge and filled her bowl.

"True."

"And I couldn't stop thinking about it."

"Steven or Mark?"

"Both." She leaned back against the counter and ate.

Kathy took a sip of her coffee. "Why don't you try calling Steven and apologizing?"

"I already apologized. Last night. He told me not to call him until I'm ready to talk. It sounded like he might be on the edge of breaking up."

"But you have to try to fix this. You don't want to lose him over Mark Gad. That man is already responsible for ruining the lives of enough women. Don't let him add you to his list."

"I know, but what am I supposed to do? Make up with Steven and then have to hurt him again the next time we need

HARPY

to run after something related to Mark and that mess?"

The phone started ringing again.

Samantha waved the spoon at the phone on the wall. "Are you ever going to answer that? That's four times now."

"It's too early," Kathy said. "Give me some time to wake up."

Samantha stepped to the phone. "I'm about to tell him to back off."

"Don't do that!"

"So answer the phone!"

The incessant ringing only added to the noise of the morning.

"Look, he has a class at 10:30," Kathy said. "The phone calls will stop soon. Just ignore it until then. Let's get off the topic of the men in our lives and talk about someone else: Mark."

"Another man in our lives." Samantha raised the bowl to her lips and sipped up the rest of the milk.

"Not by choice," Kathy corrected. "We need to find him and make sure the harpies haven't gotten to him."

On the way home from Mark's office, they drove by his house to make sure he was home. There were two cars in the driveway, which meant that he had made it home okay. Judging by their brief encounter with Tina Gad, they both speculated that she would've called the police if Mark hadn't returned home.

"He's not the one I'm worried about," Samantha said. "It's the other potential victims the harpies will go after to make up for not getting Mark."

"Right, but what if Mark is really deserving of getting taken away?"

Samantha shook her head. "Not our call."

"We don't even have the whole story," Kathy countered. "We figured out from that court document we found in Mark's desk yesterday that the people suing him are Robert and Debra Powers. That's probably the girl's parents."

"Well, after thinking about it all night, I've realized that we don't know that for sure," Samantha said. "Best not to get involved before we know for sure."

"But it's a lead."

"And what if we spot the harpies? We should be coming up with a way to stop them."

"I'll look in the attic and see if there are any brass instruments up there. Maybe someone in our family has dealt with harpies before."

"We need a spell or a potion or something."

Kathy shook her head. "I'm not sure there's one that will stop them."

"Maybe a banishment spell then. If we can't kill them, then let's get them the hell away from Erie."

"I still think we should look into what happened with the Powers girl."

Samantha rolled her eyes and pulled the phone book out of the cabinet beside the phone. "Fine, if it'll make you feel better,

I'll look them up and talk to them just to prove to you that they're not who we should be focusing on."

"Not with that attitude, you're not! They lost their daughter to suicide. Think of what they're going through."

Samantha studied her sister and open her mouth to reply when the phone started ringing again. "That's it!" She snatched it up and said into it with a bite to her voice, "Yes?"

"No!" Kathy grimaced once she realized it was too late.

Samantha's demeanor changed in an instant. "Oh, Mr. Marsden, hi."

Kathy's eyes went wide and she tried to communicate with her sister simply by looking at her, but Samantha turned away.

The older sister's hand went to the back of her neck to smooth out the many fly-away hairs. "No, this isn't a bad time. Have you put together a panel?"

Kathy stared as her sister talked, hoping she could glean the direction of the phone call by only one side of the conversation. As hard as she tried, she couldn't make out what Mr. Marsden was saying on the other end.

"Really?" Samantha turned and gave a thumbs up. "That's wonderful! Of course, I accept! Thank you!"

Kathy cheered quietly in her seat, feeling relief that at least one of them was getting their life together. Not that she ever doubted that her sister would.

Samantha moved to the calendar on the wall. "Uh, the 27th works for me. Is there anything I need to bring?" She listened and nodded. "Okay, sounds good. I'll bring those with me then. Thank you so much!"

"Well?" Kathy said as Samantha hung up the phone.

"I got the job!" she cheered.

Kathy jumped to her feet and hugged her sister. "Congratulations, Sam! I'm so proud of you!"

"Thank you. I guess whatever I said in the interview really impressed him because he said the more he thought about it the more he realized he wanted me for the job, so he decided to skip the panel interview and offer it to me right away."

"That's awesome. So you start next week?"

Samantha nodded. "Which means I need to start building up my wardrobe."

"Hey, I am down for a trip to the mall." Kathy was glad to see how happy her sister was, especially with everything that happened with Steven the night before.

"Oh, and I need to get some of my paperwork together and figure out how long it'll take me to get there so I know what time to wake up and—"

"Isn't there someone you should call first?"

Samantha made a face. "I know. I want to. I just don't want Steven to feel like I'm only seeing him when it's convenient."

"Sam, he loves you. He knows that's not the case. He'd be mad if you *didn't* tell him."

"Yeah."

"So call him and go celebrate and make everything okay."

HARPY

Samantha looked down at the phone book. "What about the Powers'?"

"I'll call them and figure out a way to talk to them to get the scoop on their daughter and their beef with Mark," Kathy said. "We'll figure out a plan from there."

"Okay." Samantha nodded and then hugged her sister again. "Thanks, Kathy. You're my best friend."

"Aw, that's what I'm here for."

"I'm going to go get ready." She started to leave the room, but stopped and turned. "Before either of us go anywhere, do you mind checking the attic for those horns? I want us to be prepared in case the harpies decide to rain on my parade some more."

Kathy smiled. "Sure, I'll dig through the attic for them. Hopefully we have something small. I don't want to be lugging around a tuba or anything. I'd be winded before I could even blow in the stupid thing."

CHAPTER 20

Kathy tapped the bell of the small tarnished brass horn sitting on the kitchen table as the phone rang in her ear. Before Samantha left for Steven's, Kathy was able to rummage up two of the instruments, proving her theory that someone in their family had previously dealt with these creatures before.

She wondered if their ancestors had to make the same decision as they did: whether to let the victim be taken or to put a stop to the harpies snatching him. Kathy didn't feel right protecting the guilty, but it wasn't up to her to play God.

"Hello?"

Kathy was startled when the woman's voice suddenly sounded in her ear.

"Yes, hi, my name is Kathy Walker and I was wondering if you had a minute to talk?"

"We're not interested in purchasing anything over the phone."

"No, I'm not selling anything," Kathy said quickly. "You said 'we.' Is your husband there too?"

"Who is this?" the woman asked.

"My name is Kathy," she repeated. "Is this Debra? Debra Powers?"

"What is this? Who are you with?"

"No one, ma'am. I just want to talk."

"I'm hanging up," Debra said. "If you call me again, I'm calling the police."

"Ma'am, I just want to talk to you about your lawsuit against Mark Gad," Kathy nearly shouted to catch her before she hung up.

It was quiet on the other end, but there was no dial tone so Kathy knew that she had Debra's attention.

"The lawsuit's about your daughter, isn't it? Her suicide—"

"How did you find out about that?" Debra snapped. "Are you working for that man? Did he hire a private investigator? I can tell you right now, if that's the case you're not very good at your job."

"No, I'm not a private investigator," Kathy said. "I just want to help. I think it's unfair that your daughter died over something Mark put her through."

The woman's voice softened. "Oh."

"I can't imagine everything you and your husband are going through."

"Yes, it's been…it's been hard."

"I just want to hear from you what happened," Kathy said. "But I don't want to talk about something like this on the phone. Would you be willing to meet? Somewhere public, if that'll make you feel better. You can bring your husband."

The woman was quiet for a moment as she considered. Finally, she said, "Well, Robert is working. I'll think about it and maybe we can meet you tonight—"

"No, please, this is something that I don't think can wait until tonight." Kathy wasn't sure when the next harpy attack would be. Another Jeffrey Jackson could be taken before the end of the day if they didn't hurry.

"Well…"

"Can you meet me at…" Kathy racked her brain for a good place to meet. "The public library? The one downtown. Say, in, like, half an hour?"

Debra sighed heavily on the phone. "I'm not sure I'm entirely comfortable with this."

"I know, and I hate to ask this, but trust me, I wouldn't be bringing it up if it wasn't important," Kathy said. "I believe this could make a difference in saving someone else's life."

"You're making it very hard to say no."

Harpy

Kathy smiled. "Then I guess I'll see you in a bit. I'll meet you by the front door of the library in half an hour."

She waited until she heard Debra say, "Okay. I'll be there."

CHAPTER 21

Tara Lancer sat at her kitchen table with the phone pressed against her face, burning with rage.

"You took my car all day long, Derek!" she shouted into the phone. "You didn't bring it back on time and you didn't fill it up. *And* you were smoking in there! You know I hate that shit!"

"Babe, I apologized for that already," Derek said on the other end.

"Apologies don't mean shit to me, D. Don't do it again or we're done."

"Obviously apologies don't mean shit to you."

"What's that supposed to mean?"

"How's Carlos doing?" he asked.

HARPY

Carlos Rodriguez, who she'd hooked up with last weekend when she was mad at Derek for ditching her.

Tara clucked her tongue. "That's different."

"How?"

"You were pissing me off."

"So it's okay for you to cheat on me but I can't borrow your car?"

"Damn right."

"That's not fair."

"I have my own rules," she said with a giggle. "You knew what you were getting into when you got with me, so don't pretend like you don't know."

"You know, I'm tired of this."

"I don't see you leaving."

"What if I did?"

She rolled her eyes and clucked her tongue again. "Boy, you lie."

"You gotta stop disrespecting me, T."

"Then start paying my gas bill," she said. "Listen, I got my own job. I pay my own bills. I don't need to be paying yours too. That's not what I'm about."

Derek groaned. "Whatever, man."

"Check yourself and call me when you've figured it out," she said. "I ain't got time for *boys*. I'm out here looking for a grown-ass *man*." She slammed the phone down in the cradle and chuckled to herself. "Idiot."

DAVID NETH

The phone started ringing again. She picked up the receiver and slammed it back down again. She knew it was Derek calling back. She wasn't going to play his games.

The phone rang yet again, so she got up and went out onto her front porch. It was getting stuffy in her kitchen anyway. She needed some fresh air to calm her down.

Out on the porch, she waved to the neighbor, a man who was living with his girlfriend and their baby daughter. But Tara didn't mind if he didn't mind. As far as she was concerned, she and Derek were done. And she had only gotten with Carlos to make Derek mad.

Tara stretched, raising her arms in the air, feeling her shirt lift up to reveal her belly. Anything to get the attention of the neighbor. He was a father. That was a real man.

He leaned against his car and bit his bottom lip, watching her.

Hook, line, and sinker.

Tara walked down the steps of her porch and started crossing the street when something in the air caught her eye. Three somethings. They looked like birds but…different. She squinted against the sun, trying to decipher what it is they were, but she couldn't figure it out.

As they got closer, she saw that they looked like people…with wings. She shook her head and blinked, trying to clear the spots from her eyes from looking toward the sun. That's when she noticed they were getting closer. As if they were

117

aiming for her.

Screaming, Tara took off in a run down the street, trying to get away from them. The screeches of the bird creatures told her they were following her.

Hunting her.

CHAPTER 22

Samantha knocked on Steven's door, worrying that they were about to have another argument. She also realized on the drive over here that nothing had really changed much since last night. The only differences were that they both had time to cool off and Samantha was now employed. Would her news be enough to make up for crashing their date? She hoped it would.

He answered the door in a white T-shirt and jeans. "Oh, Sam, hi."

"Hi," she said sheepishly. "Can I come in?"

Steven considered for a moment and then stepped back and swept his arm out, gesturing for her to come inside.

He lived near the end of Parade Street in an apartment

HARPY

house on the first floor. It was a very clearly hastily converted into a duplex. His unit was technically only one bedroom, but the living room and kitchen were large, indicating they were original to the house's floor plan. Likewise, most of the original trim work remained in the living room, even the spindles for the staircase that had been haphazardly blocked off for the upstairs unit. It wasn't pretty, but Samantha had to admit that Steven kept it as nice as he could for what he had to work with.

"Sorry I didn't call—actually, why aren't you at work?"

Steven offered a tight smile that told her he wasn't pleased. "Ah, you forgot that too." He leaned back against the wall, not inviting her in any further. "Part of the reason we were doing a big date day last night was because I took today off from work for a long weekend."

Samantha closed her eyes and rolled her head back, remembering it all. She had promised to spend the weekend with him. A way to savor her time off before she got a full time job and had less time for him. He had taken off of work and cooked dinner. He had made his sacrifices and Samantha was unable to make hers.

"I am *so sorry*," she said. "I've been so busy and I wish I can say that things will be different, but I can't promise that. I'm doing my best to juggle it all and I know I'm failing and I'm sorry." Her voice broke as it all hit her.

He reached for her. "Don't cry. You know I hate to see you cry."

She leaned into him and said, "I want to make it up to you. And, of course, I didn't come here to say all that. I came here to talk about me."

He held her out. "What about you? What's going on?"

She wiped at her eyes, feeling like an idiot for crying like she was. She didn't want to make up with Steven because he felt bad for her. She wanted their relationship to work.

"Not right now," she said. "We need to talk about us. I'm sorry for being a bad girlfriend lately. I've just got a lot going on. I should've respected your time and told you that before you went to all these lengths for me."

Steven took her hands and kissed her forehead before pulling her in for another hug. "I was mostly annoyed yesterday because I had this whole special weekend planned for us and it seemed like you couldn't be bothered by it. I was going to—this weekend was supposed to be special."

"So what do we do now?"

He squeezed her tighter. "I guess just be more mindful of each other. I'll check in with you more about what you've got going on and you try to keep me in the loop. How's that?"

"I think that's the best we can do." She pulled away and smiled at him. Wiping at her eyes, she said with a chuckle, "I must look like such a typical whiny girl. Ugh, I'm sorry."

He laughed. "I get it. It's okay. It's not like I'm going to make fun of you for it."

"Better not," she said. "I know where you sleep."

HARPY

"Would you like another visit to my chambers?"

"Easy," Samantha said with a smirk. "First I have something big to tell you."

"About you, right." He stood back and crossed his arms with a smile.

"*Yes*, about me," she said. "I got a call from Mr. Marsden at the CPA office today…"

His eyebrows went up. "And?"

"And they offered me the job! I start next week!"

"Samantha, that's awesome!" He wrapped her up in a hug, lifting her off her feet and planted a big kiss on her lips.

She laughed as he tossed her over his shoulder and started carrying her through the apartment to his bedroom in the back.

As she laughed and struggled to keep her head upright, she caught a glimpse of the sky out the window as the three harpies darted by.

"Put me down," Samantha told Steven, all lightness drained from her voice.

Immediately, he set her on her feet. "What's the matter?"

"I'll be back," she said, darting to the door. "Stay here!"

Racing down the rickety steps of the porch, Samantha stopped at her car to grab the brass horn sitting on the passenger seat and took off in a sprint down the middle of the street. There was a smaller chance of tripping on an uneven sidewalk or having to maneuver around another walker or a dog.

A car honked as she barreled through an intersection, but she ignored them. With her eyes locked on the harpies in the air, her arms pumping, and her fist clenched tightly around the horn, she hoped that she would make it in time to prevent someone else being carried off by the harpies.

She just needed to be fast enough.

CHAPTER 23

- FEBRUARY 1954 -

Sharon pulled the curtains closed on one of the windows overlooking Main Street and then shivered as she watched it gently waft in the draft sifting through the thin pane.

"Patrick still hasn't fixed that yet?" Dorothy asked from the dining room table. She had a burgundy sweater pulled over her shoulders and she wrapped her hands around her warm coffee.

"Not yet." Sharon retook her seat at the table across from her downstairs neighbor. Since the winter hit, they'd been getting together at least once a week to get to know each other. Sharon was grateful for her company and Dorothy quickly became her only friend in Washington.

"You two have been here almost a year!" Dorothy said with a laugh. "Doesn't the draft bother him?"

Sharon shrugged. "He's not here much. Been working a lot at the garage."

"He better be taking some time off next week for Valentine's Day. Do you two have something special planned?" Dorothy sipped her coffee. "The first one as a married couple is always one to be remembered. During our first year, Charlie sent me out shopping with a couple of my girlfriends and when I came home, he had cleaned the whole apartment, top to bottom, and cooked us a *fabulous* dinner! Oh, it was so special!"

Sharon smiled. "That's nice."

"Do you think Patrick has anything like that planned?"

Shrugging, she said, "I'm not sure. He hasn't mentioned Valentine's Day. I guess things are pretty busy down at the garage and he's been coming home pretty stressed."

Dorothy saw the sadness in her neighbor's eyes. "How are things going with you two?"

Sharon smiled, but it didn't reach her eyes. "They're okay."

"I'm only asking because I know there are often…growing pains during the first year of a marriage," Dorothy said. "Charlie and I had our ups and downs, but we mostly had ups. Learning to live with someone you love is a challenge in and of itself! And you two moved across the state!"

"Things are okay."

Dorothy took a deep breath. "Honey, are you sure? I don't mean to pry, but I *do* live downstairs and, well, I hear things."

Sharon felt her throat go dry.

Harpy

"You two argue an awful lot, especially if you say he's not home often. From what I hear, it's not good."

"I'm sorry." Sharon felt her face grow hot, but she took a big sip of her coffee anyway to hide for a moment. "I didn't realize we were being so loud."

"No, not you, dear. Him. I hear Patrick. Honey, he says some vicious things to you. I try to ignore them as best I can, but I can't help but wonder—"

"It's fine," Sharon cut her off. "He's under a lot of stress since he's the only one with a job."

"You could get a job too."

She shook her head. "Patrick said he'd rather me be home, taking care of the apartment."

"He's your husband, that doesn't mean he *controls* you."

Sharon sat back, feeling uncomfortable. "It's fine. I don't need to get a job."

"It's not just about the job. I'm worried that he doesn't *respect* you. From what I hear of the yelling, it doesn't seem like he does."

"You've got it all wrong. Sometimes I just make him mad. It's my fault, really."

Dorothy gave her neighbor a look that said: *I don't believe you.*

"I just—I'm still learning how to be a good wife," Sharon said.

Dorothy's eyes grew wide. "Oh, sweetheart..."

"I'll learn."

"A husband and wife are supposed to complement each other," she said. "Where one fails, the other picks up the slack. Husbands and wives should be pushing each other to become better versions of themselves. Not tearing them down and belittling them."

Sharon averted her neighbor's eyes. She didn't want to hear the lecture. Didn't want to believe that what Dorothy was saying might be true.

"Ask yourself this," Dorothy went on, "do you need to be a better wife or does he need to be a better husband?"

In response, Sharon shrugged. There had been moments where she wished Patrick was different. More loving. More helpful. More appreciative of everything she did around the house. She might not have a job, but she provided a home for him to come back to and relax in.

Sometimes, when things got bad and no one was around, she worried that she made a mistake in marrying him.

"Sharon, sweetheart, I'm only saying all of this because I care about you and I want the best for you. Now, I won't stand for you being pushed around by someone who claims he loves you. You need to draw the line and say something to him. Let him know that you demand his respect."

"That won't work."

"Have you even tried?"

"Of course I've tried!" Sharon nearly shouted. They were

both quiet in the aftermath of her eruption. "I'm sorry for snapping."

"Don't apologize," Dorothy said. "I think we're finally getting somewhere. Now go on. Say what you need to say."

"Every time I try to put my foot down, he...pushes back harder."

Dorothy stared at her neighbor as realization came over her. "Are you saying he hits you?"

Sharon shrugged. "Sometimes—but it's only when I do something to make him mad. There's always a reason."

"No!" Now it was Dorothy's turn for an outburst. "There's *never* a reason for a man to hit his wife. Sharon, honey, you're not a wife, you're a captive. You deserve better."

"And what do you want me to do about it? We're married, it's done."

Dorothy fidgeted with the napkin under her coffee mug. She had nearly forgotten about the chill coming through the windows. Her blood was boiling as she learned everything that happened in the apartment above her. "You know, it's becoming more and more acceptable for women to...get divorced."

"And then what?" Sharon asked. "I have no skills, no job, and I'm as far away from my family as possible. How am I supposed to support myself?"

"Sweetie, there are people who will help take care of you—"

Sharon got to her feet and pointed to the door. "Please leave."

"I didn't mean to offend you. Like I said, I'm only saying all of this because I care about you."

"You don't even know me," Sharon said. "We haven't known each other long and you've made assumptions about me and my husband that are hurtful. I didn't ask for your marriage advice. So please leave my apartment."

"Sharon—"

"Go!"

Rising, Dorothy started toward the door, but turned around before she exited. "Let me just say this: I want you to at least think about everything I've said. You deserve to be happy. And I don't believe that you are." Turning, she stepped out and closed the door behind her.

Sharon folded her arms across her chest and stared at the door. Her head was spinning, going over everything Dorothy had said. Most prominent of all was the worry in her voice: Maybe she's right.

CHAPTER 24

"A re you Kathy?" A dark-haired woman walked up the stone steps to the front door where Kathy was waiting under the ornate awning outside the library.

Instinctively, Kathy smiled, tucked the small brass horn under her arm, and approached the woman with an outstretched hand. "Debra? Hi. It's nice to finally meet you."

Debra nodded and returned a sad smile. Kathy could see the wrinkles on the woman's face emphasized by her constant worry. The pain of losing her daughter evident through the smile.

"Are you in a band?" she asked, indicating the horn.

Kathy scrunched up her face. "Well…not exactly. It's just, um, I took the bus down here and I'm going to drop this off to

130

get it, uh, cleaned after our meeting."

Debra nodded, still suspicious.

"Let's go inside and find a quiet place to sit," Kathy suggested.

They entered and crossed the marble-clad Main Hall to the Fiction Room and found a pair of comfortable chairs in the corner, away from anyone else. The last thing Kathy wanted was for Debra to be nervous about sharing her story due to eavesdroppers.

"It's gorgeous in here," Kathy started, looking around. She set the horn down on a nearby table. "I used to love to come in here and just look around. Actually, sometimes I still do that when my boyfriend—"

"I don't want to come off as rude, Kathy, but I'm not here for small talk," Debra cut in. "To be honest, I'm not even sure why I'm here. I guess it's because you seemed genuine on the phone, but now that I'm here I'm not sure—"

"I promise you, I'm not fishing for gossip. I just want to know the story. I have reason to believe someone wants to hurt Mark Gad."

Debra rolled her eyes. "He deserves whatever's coming to him."

Kathy bit her bottom lip, debating how to navigate through this woman's rightful hatred for the man.

"Not that we hired anyone to hurt him," Debra added. "My husband and I just couldn't stand the fact that we're grieving our daughter while the man responsible for her death is walking free. That's part of the reason we filed the lawsuit, hoping that he'd pay *somehow* to make up for what we lost." She pulled a tissue out of her purse and dabbed at her eyes. "Not that any amount of money would make up for losing Linda. And we only filed because Mark took it to that level, threatening to sue us for defamation or something absurd like that."

Kathy's head was spinning from everything Debra was saying. "Wait, why don't you start from the beginning? When Mark and Linda first met."

Debra sat back in her chair and crossed her legs. "I'm afraid I don't know the whole story. It seems the only one who does is Mark and he's certainly not going to say anything."

"Okay, so why don't you tell me what you saw, then?"

She cleared her throat and looked down at her fidgeting hands, kneading the crumpled tissue. "Linda was our world. After being told my husband and I wouldn't be able to conceive, Linda came along and proved all those doctors wrong. She was the answer to our prayers and everything we ever dreamed of." She swallowed hard. "But Linda had some…struggles."

"What kind of struggles?"

"Depression, mostly," Debra said. "I don't believe—well, what happened…at the end, uh, had anything to do with that, though."

"Why not?"

"Linda was getting better. Seeing a therapist, he had her on a prescription that seemed to be working. She had drive again. She was hanging out with her friends again, talking about starting dance again. Everything she loved but gave up when her depression got really bad."

"So where does Mark come in?"

"I don't know exactly when or how they met, but she started to change."

"Change how? Good or bad?"

Debra shrugged. "I can't really say. We just noticed she…wasn't herself. And I don't think it had anything to do with her depression or the medication she was on, because she continued to take those, as far I know. She just stopped hanging out with her friends, put off filling out the application to rejoin dance until it was too late for the season. But she was her happy, healthy self. So her father and I weren't too concerned. We just thought she was growing up and her interests were changing."

"How long ago was that?"

"Maybe a year ago, I think."

Kathy nodded.

"One day her father flat-out asked her if she had a boyfriend—they would talk about things like that all the time. She was such a daddy's girl."

"What did she say?"

Debra nodded. "That she did have a boyfriend. Robert asked when we could meet him and she didn't seem like she wanted us to, which concerned us. Then shortly after that, her whole attitude changed. She was angry, crying, stopped taking her meds, refused to go to therapy."

Kathy raised her eyebrows, but didn't say anything.

Debra noticed her expression and added, "We finally convinced her to go back and get everything straightened out, but you have to understand, with medication like that it takes a while for things to set in and really work. Her hormones and chemicals and whatever else were all out of balance from abruptly stopping the medication for a while and then abruptly going back on."

"So if her and Mark broke up before you and your husband met him, how do you know she was even seeing Mark Gad?"

"Because while we were working on getting her back on her meds, the phone calls started," Debra explained. "Linda always insisted on taking them, even though the conversations they had only made things worse. The one time he called, Robert lost his temper and told him that he needed to stop harassing our daughter."

"I take it he didn't listen."

Debra shook her head. "No. We thought he did at first, but then we caught him in Linda's bedroom—they were just talking, but it was enough to startle us. We didn't realize Mark was so...so much *older*."

Nearly your age, Kathy thought to herself. *This guy is a total creep.*

"My husband lost it again and nearly assaulted him. I

couldn't blame him. I wanted to do the same thing myself. But we both quickly saw the state the whole scene had on Linda so we told him to never come back again and to leave her alone." Debra swallowed hard. "She told us he had been sneaking over to see her when we weren't home. Lord knows what he said to her..."

Kathy let the woman collect herself for a moment before pushing for more. "How long did it last before he started bothering her again?"

Debra shook her head and tears clouded her eyes again. Her lip trembled and she said, "I don't know. Shortly after that I walked in her room and...she was hanging from the ceiling fan." She bent over and covered her mouth as the sobs came, echoing throughout the quiet library.

Kathy leaned forward and rubbed Debra's back to try to comfort her. She felt the lump in her throat as she empathized with the woman, yet felt the guilt for protecting a man who led Linda Powers to killing herself.

Kathy wondered if she was even doing the right thing by saving him.

CHAPTER 25

Samantha chased the harpies down East 2nd Street, watching as they soared through the air. Up ahead, she caught sight of a woman around her age running down the sidewalk, looking behind her every so often with panic in her eyes.

She just needed to get to her and then she could fend off the harpies. Maybe even get an explanation out of them, or possibly even make a deal so they would stop killing people.

Her hand was getting sweaty from its grip on the brass horn. She considered blowing it to ward off the harpies, but they were too far away to hear it. If she was going to pause long enough to blow into it, she wanted to make sure it would do its job.

The woman crossed German Street and darted across

several empty lots leftover from house demolitions. Samantha made it to the sidewalk before the harpies shifted downward, aiming right at the woman. They struck her before she could make it to the cover of the trees.

"NO!" Samantha shouted, ignoring the cramp in her side as she sprinted across the space. With adrenaline pumping, she used the last of the air in her lungs to blow into the brass horn.

That caught their attention.

All three harpies looked back at Samantha, who blew the horn again. Their feathers ruffled and as Samantha raised the horn to her lips a third time, the harpies took off, leaving their latest victim in the grass.

Samantha rushed to the woman's side.

"Is she hurt?" someone from the street called to Samantha.

"Call 9-1-1!" Samantha dropped to her knees beside the woman who had been running. She had several large gashes across her stomach and tears in her eyes. Blood was everywhere, but her chest continued to rise and fall frantically.

"Miss, we're getting help for you," Samantha told her. "Hang in there."

The woman nodded weakly, her eyelids drooping.

Samantha scanned the woman's body, worrying what she could do. There were too many gashes to even try to stop the bleeding. Pressing on one would force more blood out of another. Instead, she turned the woman's head to her. "Hey, look at me. Keep your eyes on me."

137

Harpy

"They're on their way!" the woman from behind said. Moments later, she was beside Samantha.

The witch stood and pointed down to the woman. "Make sure she keeps her eyes on you and stays awake. We need to get something to stop the bleeding." Maybe if they had multiple people applying pressure, there was a chance. The doubt in Samantha's mind said otherwise.

Samantha looked in the sky, trying to catch sight of the harpies. She wanted to tear them apart with her bare hands.

The woman from the street, who was knelt down beside the woman on the ground, said, "She's not breathing."

Samantha's head snapped around. She dropped down on the other side and tried to get the woman to wake up, shaking her, talking to her, and finally yelling at her. But it wasn't enough.

"Dammit!" Samantha shouted. Then a thought hit her and she looked at the other woman kneeling, who had tears in her eyes. "Did you know her?"

"What?"

"Did you know her? What's her name?"

"Uh...I don't know! She lived around the corner, I think. I saw her walking her dog a couple times. Why?"

"What was her home life like? Did she have any demons she was fighting? Get into any arguments?" Samantha wanted to know if the harpies had a reason for attacking this woman or if they were hunting down perfectly innocent people now.

"What are you talking about?"

Rising to her feet, Samantha caught sight of Steven running toward her but she ignored him and darted to the houses across the street. She raced up the front porch of one house and pounded her fist on the front door, trying to get someone to answer.

Before anyone came to the door, Steven had finally caught up with Samantha and wrapped his arms around her, pulling her back to the sidewalk.

"Shh, easy, Sam," he said into her ear. "You did what you could. The police are on their way. Whoever did this will be found."

Feeling his arms around her, reality set in. That she was too late. That the harpies had escaped again. That she had yet another reason to lie to Steven. And that she was being irrational, hysterical even.

Giving in, she leaned into him and let it all come out until they both sunk to the sidewalk as she sobbed in his arms.

CHAPTER 26

- APRIL 1954 -

A re you ready to go?" Patrick asked when he came out of the hotel bathroom.

Sharon stood at the window and looked out over the city. From up on the eighth floor, everyone looked so small, moving around on the sidewalk. She watched as a streetcar stopped at an intersection at the end of the block and people piled out onto the sidewalk before more moved in to take their place.

The sky was overcast, which was typical for mid-April. Not to mention the fact that Pittsburgh was known as the "Smoky City." She could feel the chill in the air, the dampness it contained, just by looking out over the skyline. People were still bundled up in coats and moving with purpose in a way you do when the weather makes you want to go inside.

"Sharon, baby, are you listening?" Patrick came over and wrapped her in a hug. It took everything in her not to push him away.

He had insisted on spending a weekend in Pittsburgh for their first anniversary. On one hand, she couldn't believe it had only been a year, but at the same time she felt like their marriage had been a lifetime. A life sentence.

Ever since she had her talk with Dorothy, Sharon slowly started to take more control in her marriage in ways that were within Patrick's allowance. She didn't spend as much time cleaning the house. She ventured throughout town and took up hobbies that he knew nothing about—joining a book club at the library or volunteering at Washington Hospital as a candy striper. Most of all, she began to pull away from Patrick. Just as Dorothy said, if he wasn't going to respect her, he didn't deserve her attention.

"Do we have to go?" she asked. "It's kind of gloomy out."

"We have tickets to a show waiting for us at the box office. I called ahead for them."

"Well, I don't feel like going." She took a seat on the edge of the bed and crossed her arms.

He huffed, but didn't otherwise get angry. His temper had been a little better since she'd been pulling away. He likely noticed that she wasn't going to be pushed around anymore. And yet she was still here, still his wife, so there were moments that his former self slipped through.

Okay, he was a lot like his former self. Only the outbursts were fewer than they were before. He seemed to try to stop himself before lashing out at her. Sharon wondered if he was having an affair and was surprised to realize that the thought of that didn't even bother her.

Let some other woman take him off my hands, she thought.

Patrick looked at his watch. "It's just after four. The show doesn't start until six. Let's go out, walk around for a little bit, find the theater, and then if you still don't feel like going we can just go to dinner. We have to eat at some point, right?"

She sighed because he had a point. They would have to leave the hotel room at some point. And the more time they spent out and about, the less chance there was that he would turn into his nasty self.

"Fine. Let's go."

Patrick grabbed a page he had ripped out of the hotel phone book and brought it with him. Down in the lobby, he asked the hotel clerk for directions to Loew's Penn Theatre, which was right at the end of the block.

Once they got to the theater and waited in line at the box office, Sharon realized that instead of taking her to a stage production, Patrick had opted for a Hollywood film. Something they could've seen back in Washington. He probably chose it over a stage production because it was cheaper. Money was always the driver behind his actions.

"Wait a minute, that's not the price I was told over the phone," Patrick argued with the young man behind the counter. "Why did it jump up so high?"

"These are the day-of ticket costs," the man explained.

"I only called yesterday! They didn't tell me anything about a price gouge like this! This is unacceptable!"

"Patrick, easy," Sharon said. *So much for Patrick being different. At least he's not yelling at me.*

"You shut your mouth!" he shouted at her.

And there it is.

Turning back to the man behind the counter, he said, "I'm trying to take my wife out on a nice date for our anniversary and you try to rip me off like this. Forget that, I'll pay what I was told over the phone."

The man behind the counter was defiant. "No, sir. That is not the price of the day-of tickets."

"Is there a problem here?" A large man stepped into the lobby and approached Patrick and Sharon.

"Yeah, this asshole is trying to price gouge my tickets!"

"Sir, this young man doesn't control the price of the tickets," the man said. "Only sells them. If you would like to speak with the manager, I would happily offer you his phone number."

"Phone number?" Patrick shouted. "I want to speak to him now! Get him out here! I'm not leaving until I get those tickets at the price I deserve."

"Patrick, it's really not that big of a deal," Sharon muttered and took hold of his arm.

He shrugged her off and turned his anger to the man. "Don't just stand there like an idiot. Get the manager, like you said!"

"Sir, if you don't change your tone, I'm going to have to ask you to leave."

"And who the hell are you to ask me to leave?"

The man puffed out his chest. "I'm the chief of security for Loew's. And with the way you're acting, I'm afraid I'm going to have to escort you out."

Patrick shrugged off the man's attempts to grab him. "You're not taking me anywhere."

The security guard took a firm grip of Patrick's elbow and led him and Sharon to the door. "Either you go willingly or I call the police."

"All right! I'm going, I'm going!" Patrick shook off the guard's hand and followed Sharon out onto the sidewalk. "Geez, you think you're the only theater in town! I'll take my money elsewhere!"

"Patrick, let's just go and get something to eat and forget about this."

"Of course you'd say that!" he shouted at her, which surprised her. Other than just now in the lobby, he had never snapped at her in public before. Always hidden his anger for the *comfort* of their own home. "You never wanted to go in the first place."

Sharon bit her tongue. No matter what she said, it'd be wrong and he'd have a comeback. If she didn't say a word, he had nothing to yell at her for. It'd been her strategy the last two months and it helped her gain some ground in their marriage.

Without another word to her, Patrick stalked off down the street, deeper into downtown. Sharon followed because she had no other choice. She was in a strange city where she didn't know anyone or where anything was. And she couldn't go back to the hotel because Patrick had the key.

For the next half hour, they zigzagged through downtown, losing themselves in the network of streets. At one point, Patrick abruptly turned into a restaurant and waited for a table. Sharon quietly followed him in.

It was a seafood restaurant in an ornate building. Waiting at their table was a lit candle and rose petals scattered around the tablecloth. Sharon wondered if they could even afford it, but Patrick had made it abundantly clear that money was none of her concern or control.

Let him burn through his own money on dinner. And he says I waste it.

"I'm hungry too," she offered with a smirk. It was the first thing they'd said to each other since leaving the theater.

It was also the last thing the two of them said to each other until the meal was over and the check was paid.

"You ready?" Patrick asked. He didn't wait for a response and rose to his feet. Once they were outside, he reached for her hand like there was nothing wrong. "That was a nice meal, wasn't it?"

"The food was good," Sharon said. *And the conversation wasn't half bad—because there wasn't any.*

The sun had gone down while they were eating and now the city looked completely different. Fewer people were on the street, oil streetlamps flickered, yet in the distance they still heard the sound of cars and trolleys moving throughout the street grid. With the sun out of sight, the chill in the air was even worse and the sudden gusts of wind didn't help the situation. She thought about using her magic to help counteract the wind, but that would take concentration since she didn't use her magic often. And it would likely result in a fight if Patrick realized what she was doing.

"Do you remember the way back to the hotel?" he asked.

That took her by surprised because he had inadvertently admitted that he didn't know where he was going. The *man* was asking his *wife* for help.

Rather than point out his fault, she led him down the street, trying to get her bearings without letting on that she didn't know where they were anymore than he did.

"Third Avenue," she muttered. "Wasn't our hotel on Sixth Street? They've gotta be close. Let's go down here."

"You don't have any idea where we are, either." He finally caught on and let go of her hand. "No, I think it's down here."

He turned down a street Sharon knew for a fact led to the

riverfront, but she didn't say anything and followed him anyway. The wind was intense as they walked down the block.

"If we follow along the river, we should get back to our hotel, right?" he wondered aloud.

"Except, there's no way to walk along the whole edge of the river. It's blocked off by the train tracks we came in on." Not to mention, walking along the river would be freezing.

Patrick stopped when he saw the tracks preventing them from walking along the edge of the river. "So what do you suggest we do?"

Sharon pointed to a storefront at the end of the block. "There's a corner store. Let's go in and use their phone to call for a cab."

"I don't want to pay for a cab," he grumbled.

Because you spent too much on dinner.

"Then let's go and get a map and ask for directions," she said. "Patrick, I'm tired and cold and I just want to go to bed."

With a stony expression, he pulled out his wallet and gave her some money. "Fine. Go get your damn map."

She hurried down to the corner store and asked the shopkeeper for directions, where he told her that there was a difference between avenues and streets. Third Avenue didn't mean Third Street. They were two different places.

He helped her as best he could with the little knowledge Sharon had of where their hotel was and she left the shop with a map in hand.

HARPY

Patrick was still waiting on the corner where she left him. He had a cigarette in his mouth, which she hoped would calm him down. Not that it ever had in her experience.

"This will help," she said triumphantly as she returned with the map in hand.

"Give me that." Patrick tried to take it from her just as a gust of wind came through and blew the map out of both of their hands.

He chased after it, but another gust picked it up in the air, over the railroad tracks, and into the rushing water of the Monongahela River.

"That's money down the drain!" he snapped at her.

"If you wouldn't have fought me for it, we wouldn't have lost it!"

The back of his hand hit her before she even saw it coming.

"Don't talk to me like that! This is your fault!"

Anger overshadowed her fear. Consumed her. This was the first time he had hit her in months. And the first time he did it in public. She wasn't going to allow it.

"*You're* the one who got us lost!" she snapped. "*You're* the one on an ego trip! *You're* the one who is too petty to ask for help!"

Patrick pushed her to the ground.

"What are you going to do, Pat? Hit me? Bet you'll feel like a real man then, huh?"

He punched her in the face. Hard.

She could feel her cheek swelling, but her anger was in the driver's seat now. A year's worth of resentment from the torment and abuse she faced finally having an outlet. The rage felt good.

"What's the matter? Don't like it that your wife finally sees right through you?"

Another punch. Her left eye began to swell shut. She felt a couple of her teeth loosen, but her overwhelming rage brought out a maniacal laugh.

"Haven't learned your lesson?" He raised his fist to drive another punch to her.

Before he could make contact with her, she let out an ear-splitting screech, louder than she'd ever screamed before. Sharon jumped to her feet and her body twisted as she contorted and evolved.

Patrick watched in horror. "What the hell's the matter with you? Is this some weird witch thing?"

Feathered wings shot out of Sharon's back. Her feet bust through her boots, razor sharp with claws. Feathers burst out along her arms until her hands morphed into claws with long talons, snapping his wedding ring open and sending it skidding across the street.

"What the…?" Patrick stumbled backward, his mouth hanging open. Fear was evident across his face.

Sharon, in her new form, charged at him, swatting across his chest, drawing blood. He screamed out, called for help, but

HARPY

none came. He asked her to stop—begged her for forgiveness—but she wasn't his wife anymore. She had changed forever.

And she was going to make him pay.

After delivering enough swipes to him that he'd passed out, instinct took over and she scooped him up in her new talons, stretched her wings and flew into the night sky.

Where they were going neither of them had been before, but she knew exactly where it was. And it was exactly where Patrick belonged.

CHAPTER 27

With the small brass horn in one hand, Kathy walked out of the library with her head in the clouds. Debra had long since left and for the last half hour or so, Kathy just sat in the library, thinking about everything. How Mark tormented Linda, how Kathy was protecting Mark, and how hurt Debra was.

The whole thing left a bad taste in her mouth and a bad feeling in the pit of her stomach. She didn't know what the right answer was, but she wanted to get home to talk to Samantha about it. She worried they were making a mistake by protecting Mark from the harpies. Surely, he deserved what those creatures wanted to deliver.

She was so consumed in her own thoughts that she nearly

HARPY

collided with Jeremy as she descended the stone stairs onto the sidewalk. His backpack was over his shoulder and he was wearing a pair of sunglasses.

He held her by her arms to steady her and laughed. "I was wondering when you'd notice me. I've been watching you as I walked up."

"Oh, hi," she stammered. She wasn't expecting to see him there.

"You getting some new books or—" he pointed to the horn, "disturbing the peace?"

Embarrassed, she tried to hide the horn behind her. "Since when do you come to the library?"

"Since my room is right off the living room." He turned away from the sun to face her and shifted his glasses to the top of his head. "Michael was watching TV too loud and I thought I'd get more work done here."

"What about the library that's, you know, within *walking distance* of your house?"

"This place is nicer. What's the big deal?"

"Nothing, I guess." Kathy sighed and turned to head toward the bus station, but Jeremy caught her arm.

"Hey, what's the matter? Why didn't you answer any of my calls this morning?"

"I was sleeping."

He hooked an eyebrow. "Until ten o'clock? What's going on?"

DAVID NETH

"Oh, so you actually noticed?"

"What are you talking about?"

"Yesterday was just a hit-it-and-quit-it before you ignored me to play that stupid game with Michael," she said. "I left early and you didn't seem to care."

"Is that what this is about? I told you we would do something different this weekend!" His voice had grown louder and he noticed, so he lowered it. "Kathy, I'm sorry that you felt that I was ignoring you—"

"You *were* ignoring me," she corrected. "I didn't just feel it."

"Whatever. It doesn't matter."

"It does to me."

He bit his bottom lip to hold in his retort, but when he opened his mouth it fired out anyway, with hands waving at her for added effect. "You need to stop being so selfish. You realize I'm in college? I have work to do. Do you understand what that means? Work?"

Low blow.

"I'm sorry that I don't have time to spend with you like we used to, but you're going to have to get used to it," he went on. "If you wanted something different, all you needed to do was say so. Not pout like a little girl."

Maybe it was the emotional conversation she just had with Debra Powers or maybe it was simply the truth behind Jeremy's accusations, but Kathy felt the lump forming in her throat and forced it down. She would not let him see her cry right now.

HARPY

"If your actions weren't enough to show me you don't care, your words just sealed the deal." She felt her voice was threatening to crack, so she turned and crossed the street. By time she made it to the other side, Jeremy had run across to catch up with her.

"It's not that I don't care, Kathy," he pleaded, his tone different now that he noticed her start to falter.

"Sure seems that way to me." She kept on walking along French Street, not wanting to give him the satisfaction of her full attention. She also wanted to get on the bus as quick as possible and get back home.

"I'm sorry," he said. "Throwing that college thing at you was wrong. I know your situation is different than mine and I forget that sometimes."

His "situation" being that his family has money and Kathy's didn't. Or that his family was there and hers wasn't. Or that she was required to have a work ethic and he wasn't.

"And I know you do everything around the house while your sister's going to school," he went on. "And above all that, you're a good person."

When she reached the next crosswalk, she turned and faced him. "What's your point? Are you trying to make up with me for another five minute in-and-out *date*?"

"No, that's not—Kathy, I love you and I messed up," he said. "I didn't mean to say all that just now. I'm under a lot of stress because I screwed around for the last couple years and now I'm making up these courses and I'm having a really hard time with

154

them and if I don't pass them, I'm going to flunk out. I don't have a Plan B. This is it."

Kathy sighed. As much as she was saying he wasn't looking at things from her perspective, she wasn't looking at things from his either. She had no idea what it was like to go to college and face that kind of workload. Having a girlfriend nagging about quality time was not helping his situation.

But doing nothing and biting her tongue didn't fix their relationship.

Sensing that she was letting her guard down, Jeremy moved in tentatively for a hug. It was different from their usual embrace, but it still helped them both feel better.

When he pulled away, he caught her eye and said, "I'm sorry. I love you. And I know you probably need some time, but I'll call you later and maybe then we can talk. About whatever you want. I promise. I'll do better."

She sighed again and gave him a half smile and nodded. "Okay."

He leaned in slowly and kissed her cheek. "I'll talk to you later."

Backing away, he blew her a kiss as he headed back to the library. Kathy watched him walk away until he turned to cross the street.

Despite her anger, she knew she loved him. But apologies and promises were only the first steps to fixing things. They weren't solutions on their own.

CHAPTER 28

The bus ride home from downtown was worse for Kathy than the average ride. The afternoon sun drove the temperature up to scorching levels, which did nothing to help the stench coming off of her fellow riders who gave her curious looks as she repositioned the brass horn in her hand. Not that Kathy exactly smelled like a peach, either, with the sweat slowly dripping down her spine, but at least she had the heat to blame for her odor and not just a lack of personal hygiene.

She needed to get her own car.

Stepping off the bus was the breath of fresh air she hadn't realized she was deprived of on the trek from the heart of the city. Wiping the sweat from her brow, she finished her journey home with a two-block walk down Arlington Road from Cherry Street, where the bus had dropped her off.

She had been thinking about her argument with Jeremy the whole way home. She knew she loved him, but their relationship never seemed to fully click. There was always something off with the two of them. They had easy moments, fun moments, but there were moments when his immaturity or her lack of real-world responsibilities got in the way.

But maybe she was expecting too much. Maybe this was how relationships worked. Ebbs and flows. Maybe there was nothing wrong with the two of them and she was just reading too much into it. She really had no frame of reference, except to ask Samantha. And her sister's relationship wasn't always rock-solid itself, which, in a sick way, gave Kathy hope that everything was normal between her and Jeremy.

When Kathy finally stepped through the front door, her thoughts of Jeremy—and taking a shower to cool off and wash off the sweat—were wiped away by the stench of herbs emanating through the house. The open windows did nothing to clear the still air.

"What are you doing back here?" she asked when she stepped into the kitchen.

Samantha was behind the stove stirring a steaming, bubbling mixture in one of their oversized cast-iron pots. The kind they used to brew potions.

"Working on something to hopefully clip the wings of those

harpies, even if it's only for a short period of time," she explained. "Pass me the mullein, would you?"

Kathy looked down to where her sister was indicating and passed her the small glass jar of the dried green flecks. "Are you sure this is going to work?"

Samantha tapped some of the contents of the jar into the mixture and handed it back to Kathy. "I hope so. Those creatures killed someone else today."

"They did? Who?"

"A woman. I don't know who she was exactly," she said. "I saw them when I was at Steven's and chased them down as best I could. They're fast. The woman was terrified. She didn't seem to have any idea why she was being attacked."

Even though Samantha tried to put on a face of anger, Kathy could tell it bothered her in a different way. She lost someone and that would take its toll. Not that Kathy could blame her sister. She was having similar feelings herself about the situation.

"Were *you* able to figure out why she was attacked?" Kathy asked.

Samantha stared into the pot as she continued to stir, her face unreadable. "No. Someone called 9-1-1 and Steven was there and…yeah, it was bad. I didn't get a chance to talk to anyone or even learn the girl's name."

"I'm sorry."

"So now I want to stop these harpies long enough to ask

them what the hell they want," Samantha went on. "Maybe we could get some answers out of *them*."

"We know what they want. Mark Gad."

"Yeah. He called me today. Apparently they were watching his house."

"The harpies?" Kathy asked. "I take it they didn't do anything to him, though."

"No. He just said he saw them when he got home, he barricaded himself in the house, but they didn't go after him."

"Weird."

"I know. I tried to convince him to take our help, but he kind of brushed me off."

"So then why call you?" Kathy asked.

"I think he thinks we can control them or something."

"As much as he deserves it, no."

"Exactly," Samantha said. "I just couldn't figure out why they've only been watching him and not attacking him."

"Because we stood in their way."

Samantha shook her head. "Well, they no longer seem picky about who they're going after. And if what the book says is true and they're supposed to take people back to hell to pay for their sins, they're not sticking to that M.O."

"What do you mean? They carried off Jeffrey Jackson somewhere."

"Okay, but today all they did was tear open that woman's stomach." She swallowed hard and looked away from Kathy.

"It was horrible."

They were both quiet for a while as they thought about the harpy attacks. How even though they tried, they were still only able to stop one attack: Mark Gad. And he was likely the most guilty of them all.

"Are we doing the right thing?" Kathy asked in a small voice.

"What do you mean?"

"Well, the more people we talk to, the more Mark sounds like a bad person. And here we are protecting that bad person."

"It's not up to us to decide who can live and who can't," Samantha said. "We need to do our best to save everyone. No matter what they've done."

"You might feel differently if you were the one who talked to Debra Powers today," Kathy said.

"Debra Powers?"

"She and her husband are suing Mark over their daughter's death."

"Oh." Samantha nodded. "Right. What did you find out?"

"Nothing good."

"So Mark's guilty?"

"Sounds like it," Kathy said. "From what her mother said, Linda was already depressed and when she started dating Mark things were better for her...until they weren't."

"How old was Linda?"

Kathy shrugged. "Sounded like high school age."

"Gross. The parents didn't know that?"

"Not until they broke up. Linda was upset, went off the rails, and when her parents finally started to get her back on track, Mark started calling her…"

"Ew."

"…and *visiting* her when her parents weren't around."

"This guy is a creep."

Kathy nodded. "Uh-huh. Obviously, he didn't have anything good to say to her because shortly after her parents caught him in her *bedroom*, she killed herself."

Samantha brought a hand to her mouth, even though she knew how the story ended. And even though she didn't have any kids, she couldn't imagine finding your own child like that.

"So yeah, Mark sounds guilty as hell," Kathy said. "Debra was…inconsolable. She had to call her husband to pick her up because she was so emotional she couldn't drive."

"Oh, I bet." Samantha turned back to the pot and absently stirred it. "This whole thing is…"

"Complicated," Kathy finished. "I get it that our job is to protect everyone, but I really don't want to protect this guy."

Samantha turned off the burner and grabbed a metal funnel and several small glass vials. "Me neither. I wouldn't feel as bad if I felt like there was justice being done for Linda."

"*Legally*, he didn't kill her."

"No, but he slept with an underaged girl and played with her emotions. Not to mention, there's no telling what he was saying to her before her parents caught them."

HARPY

"Can't prove any of that," Kathy said. "Especially him sleeping with her. I wish we could, but since Linda's not around to make the claim, he's a free man."

"Either way, he sounds pretty guilty to me." Samantha finished bottling the vials. "I want to have a chat with him and hear his bogus explanation for what he did. Enough getting the story from everyone else. I want to hear it from him."

"You want to make him squirm, don't you?" Kathy smirked.

Samantha shrugged. "Hey, we might have to protect him, but that doesn't mean we need to go easy on him."

"Do you think we're actually going to track him down this time?"

"If he's not at his office or at home, we're going to have to start knocking down doors until we find him." Samantha gathered up the vials and passed two to her sister. "We can't put this off anymore. Other people are *dying* because of him."

Kathy followed her sister through the house to the front door. With their vials stashed and their adrenaline going from anger, they were ready to talk to Mark, no matter where he was hiding.

They didn't have far to look, though. When they opened the front door, Mark was stepping out of his BMW parked at the curb.

He started the walk up to the house and said, "I think we need to talk."

162

CHAPTER 29

The sisters invited Mark inside to talk, but didn't offer him to sit down like last time. Both women stood with their arms crossed and a fixed gaze on Mark.

"I, uh, take it neither one of you are very happy with the way we left things the last time we saw each other," he started. "And I just want to apologize for my accusations and threats—"

"What do you want?" Kathy asked.

"What made you decide to come back here?" Samantha added.

Mark's eyes got wide and he brought his hands to the sides of his head. "I'm going crazy. Paranoid. Those...*things* that were chasing me—the ones you two scared off—they've been lurking around me."

Harpy

"Lurking?" Samantha asked.

"Flying around my house, the office, following me home," he clarified. "I'm losing my mind, constantly worrying about when they're going to attack next."

The sisters exchanged glances. Guess the harpies didn't forget about Mark after all.

"You have to protect me," he said.

"Oh, now you want our help?" Samantha said. "After you threatened to go to the paper with an exposé on us."

"I said I was sorry. Look, I don't know what exactly you girls are into, but I know you can protect me. I need your help. Please."

Kathy noted how Mark was only making the case for himself and not for his family. Not that she was surprised by that, considering his track record.

"Why should we help you?" she asked. "We've been talking to some people about you."

That piqued his attention. "People? What people? Who are they? What are they saying?"

"I'm not going to lie, Mark," she said, "it's not great stuff."

"Who are you talking to?" he shouted, his words laced with fear.

Samantha stepped forward with a finger pointed in his face, which made Mark recoil. "*Don't* yell at us! *We* are the ones who need answers!" She pointed over to the living room. "And you're going to tell us."

He gulped, but followed her extended arm into the next room and took a seat on the couch.

The sisters followed and Samantha leaned against the arm of the chair closest to Mark while Kathy chose the spot in the chair on the other side of the room. Both sisters strategically placing themselves on either side of Mark, subtly pressuring him.

"You know, these creatures are called harpies," Samantha started.

"*Harpies*?" he asked in disbelief. "Like from mythology?"

"I think even you can state for a fact that these creatures aren't myths," Kathy said.

He nodded and stared at his hands. This was likely one of the few times he wasn't in control. Especially to women.

"Harpies only go after people who have committed horrible sins," Samantha continued. "They snatch them up and drag them off to hell to pay for those sins."

Mark didn't meet her eyes. He wrung his hands together and his right leg bounced on the hardwood.

"You wouldn't have any idea what sins you've committed, would you?" Kathy asked.

He tried to feign ease, leaning back and holding out his hands with a forced smile. "We all do bad things."

"And yet not all of us have harpies chasing after us," Kathy said.

Samantha leaned closer to Mark, focusing her persuasion

power on him. She funneled all her anger toward him into her power. "Why don't you tell us about Linda Powers."

Mark gulped and stared her. "Linda? Uh, what do you want to know?"

"Everything."

CHAPTER 30

- MARCH 1987 -

The bell above the door rang when Mark stepped into the coffee shop. Immediately, he smelled the ground coffee beans and felt a calm come over him. He always loved the ambiance of a coffee shop, especially this one, right on the corner of State Street and East 4th Street. The downtown location brought a mix of people: business men and women from nearby offices, college students spilling over from Gannon University only a block away, even a few mothers with young children coming from doctors appointments across the street.

Today, though, Mark wasn't here to people watch. He needed a strong black coffee because he was dead tired. He and Tina had been arguing the night before again. It was nearly two in the morning before they made it to bed, almost three before

167

HARPY

he fell asleep. Granted, it was in the guest room, but at least he got *some* shut-eye before his 6:00 wake-up call.

He moved to the counter, where a scrawny young man stood on the other side of the counter, adorned in a hunter green apron with the coffee shop's logo and a matching hat. The name tag pinned to the top of the apron said, "Joe" and Mark smiled at the irony.

"What can I get you?" he asked.

"A large coffee, black," Mark said, then added, "Please."

"Sure thing, boss."

As Joe turned to get Mark's drink, the bell above the door rang again and a young woman walked through the door and she made him do a double-take. She had long blonde hair and wore a gray blazer with a matching skirt. Fixing the strap of her purse on her shoulder, she stepped in line behind Mark.

"Is this place any good?" she asked him.

"I like it." He pointed to the young man getting his drink. "This guy's name is Joe, so you know they take their coffee seriously."

She laughed and touched his arm. "That's funny!"

"Are you new to Erie?" he asked.

"No, just don't adventure downtown much," she said. "I'm coming from Gannon University."

"Oh, that's a good school."

"I know," she said. "Have you been there before?"

He chuckled. Gannon was a city campus, so even if his

168

intention wasn't to go to the college, it wasn't unusual for him to pass through it on his way to somewhere else. Besides, Mark had attended shows and sporting events there through the years.

"Yeah, I've been there."

"Here you go." Joe handed him his cup and told him the price.

Mark set it down on the counter and fished his wallet out of his pocket. "You can go ahead and add hers to my bill too."

The girl's eyes lit up. "Really? Thanks!"

"Don't mention it."

"What will you have?" Joe asked her.

"A caramel cappuccino," she said, then added quickly, "small."

"You got it." Joe turned to fix her drink.

"Thank you so much," she said.

"I told you not to mention it," he said with a smirk before taking a sip of his own coffee. It was strong, but it's what he needed after the night he had. "I'm Mark."

She shook his hand and said, "Linda."

"Nice to meet you."

"You don't have to run back to the school or anything, do you?" she asked.

The school? Mark tried, but failed, to stifle his smile. Linda must've thought he was a student. He pulled his sleeve back to look at his watch. He was already half an hour late to work, but he had the time stacked up. And after the last twenty-four hours, he needed a conversation with someone that would make him feel good.

"No, I should have time."

"Do you want to sit and chat?" she asked. "It's the least I could do since you paid for mine."

Mark hesitated, while at the same time he unconsciously slid his left hand into his pocket. Slowly, he worked his wedding ring off. Linda must not have noticed it yet. "That'd be nice."

When Joe brought over Linda's order and Mark paid, the two of them sat together at a table by the window overlooking the street. Not once did either of them notice the indentation on Mark's ring finger, leftover from his wedding ring. They were too busy smiling and laughing, looking into each other's eyes.

All the while, the ring that once occupied that finger sat safely in Mark's pocket, to be slid on again once he was on his way home to his wife.

CHAPTER 31

So is that when you started seeing Linda?" Samantha asked.

Mark looked at her and then sucked in a deep breath before moving on with the rest of his story. "Yeah, we…started a relationship."

"Didn't your wife have a problem with that?" Kathy asked.

Samantha glared at her sister for breaking the connection with her power and Mark.

"I had been unhappy in my marriage for a while when I met Linda," he said.

"So talk to your wife about it," Kathy said. "Don't jump in bed with the first underaged girl you meet."

"Hey! I didn't know she was underaged until afterward," Mark barked at her.

HARPY

Samantha raised her hands to each of them. "Kathy, please? Mark, look at me."

Slowly, he turned back to her.

She pushed her power toward him. "Then what happened?"

"Well, she started getting more serious. And…" Mark hesitated, likely fighting Samantha's persuasion. "…it was very obvious she wasn't in college."

"How so?"

"She lived with her parents. Her bedroom had boy band posters and pictures of a bunch of kids with braces and she had her biology book on her desk and—"

"Her parents didn't have any concerns about you being alone with her in her room?" Samantha asked.

His shoulders tucked up briefly. "Her parents didn't know I was there."

Samantha breathed in a deep breath and suppressed all other reactions. "Did your age ever come up between you and Linda?"

"No…not until I told her I was married."

"She didn't notice that you don't look her age?" Kathy asked. "Or, you know, the wedding ring?"

"I took it off when I was with her."

She scoffed.

"Look, you don't know what it's like to be in an unhappy marriage, okay?"

Samantha waved in her own direction, trying to get him to refocus. "What did Linda say when you told her about your wife?"

"She got mad. *Really* mad. She was fuming. Kicked me out, in tears, hysterics. Teenagers, you know?"

Kathy gagged, but Samantha ignored it.

"But you didn't leave her alone, did you?"

He looked down at his hands. "We were good together. I wanted things to go back to the way they were. But she wouldn't listen to me. So I thought I'd be persistent, show her how much I cared for her because I wasn't going away."

"Were you aware of the fact that she was taking medication for depression?" Samantha asked.

"I knew she had…troubles…"

"So you didn't think there was anything wrong with calling her several times a day and showing up at her house uninvited?"

"I was trying to win her back," he said. "But then…things started getting better with Tina and I didn't want Linda to ruin it."

"You wanted to keep her quiet," Kathy said.

He shrugged.

"Did you tell Linda that you were getting back with your wife?" Samantha asked.

"Technically, we never officially separated—"

"Answer the question!" Samantha nearly shouted.

173

HARPY

"I didn't want Linda to tell anyone that we were...together," he said. "I knew I could get in trouble, potentially even go to jail, even though Linda was okay with everything. I think she knew all along that I was older, but—"

"What did you say to her?" Samantha was in no mood to hear anymore of this man's excuses.

"I told her that she needed to keep our affair quiet or else..." He scrunched his face, trying to fight Samantha's magic. "Or else I'd sue her for defamation."

"You realize she committed suicide, right?" Kathy said.

"Kathy," her sister warned.

"I didn't—"

"Your harassment pushed her to do it," she went on.

"That's not—"

Kathy continued, "Basically, you're the one who killed her."

The front doors burst open and the three harpies came swooping in. They made a beeline for Mark, but Samantha—despite her anger with him—knocked him to the floor to protect him. Instead, the bird-woman's attack tore into the couch.

Kathy got to her feet and put up her hands to freeze them, but one harpy snatched Samantha and dragged her deeper into the house while another grabbed Mark's leg and started pulling him toward the door. The third sparred with Kathy, ready to lunge at her if she decided to intervene.

Mark screamed loudly as the harpy dragged him to the

front door and the sound of Samantha's struggles could be heard from the dining room. Meanwhile, the harpy in the living room swatted at Kathy, who jumped and kicked the creature in the midsection.

It clawed at her leg, scraping her skin, but she was able to get her foot free of the creature's grasp. Remembering the potion, she fished in her pocket for the vial, but was knocked to the floor before she could use it.

Squirming under the creature's grasp to avoid any attacks, she fought to bring her feet up under it and kick it off across the room.

Scrambling to her feet, Kathy ran to her sister and threw the potion at her attacker. The harpy let go of its hold of Samantha and screeched, alerting the other two.

Kathy ran to the foyer to help kick off the harpy attacking Mark, but the screech sent the other two flying into the sky without any hostages.

With her chest heaving, Kathy ran back at her sister, who had pinned the one harpy to the floor.

"You okay?" she asked.

"A little banged up, but I'm okay," Samantha said. "Help me get her into a chair. We have more questions that need to be answered."

Together, the sisters got the creature into one of the dining room chairs and Samantha bound its arms and legs.

"Where's Mark?" she asked once the harpy was secure.

HARPY

Kathy turned back to the front door and didn't see him. She looked out onto the street and his car was gone.

"He took off again."

CHAPTER 32

The sisters stepped into the living room once they were sure the harpy was tied up securely. Samantha stood with her back to the doorframe and her eyes on the harpy while Kathy stood just out of sight of their captive.

"So what do we do now?" the younger sister asked. "The person we're supposed to be protecting is once again out of our hands and two of the creatures who are after him are out there searching for him."

Samantha shook her head, still keeping her eyes on the harpy. She kept her voice low so they couldn't be overheard. "I don't think they'll go after Mark without their third."

"What makes you so sure?"

"They've always been a trio," she explained. "Whenever we

interrupted them and separated them, they've always flown off to protect each other. They hunt in a pack and until they reconnect their pack, they're not going to hunt down Mark. They're more likely to come here first."

Kathy rolled her eyes. "Well that's reassuring."

"At least we'll know where they are."

"True. So what are we going to do about Mark? His story seemed—"

"People lie to make them feel better about themselves," Samantha cut in. "Even if they're lying to themselves. Anything to make it seem like they're not that bad. There's more to Mark's story."

"I don't know. Even his version of the facts seems like a plausible explanation for someone unstable like Linda to kill herself."

"Maybe, but I'm not sold on that story yet."

"So where do we go from here?" Kathy asked.

"We need to get the full story—and we need to find Mark."

"It's too bad we can't just let the harpies take him."

Samantha looked over at her sister. "You know we can't do that. Our powers give us a responsibility to protect—"

"—people under magical attack, yeah, yeah, yeah," Kathy droned. "I get it. I'm just not happy with it in this situation."

"Me neither. I think we'd both feel better if we knew how to end this and be done with this mess. It's now affecting more than just Mark and Linda, which never should've started to begin with."

"I can start working on a spell," Kathy said. Rhymes and cadence came to her easier than they did Samantha, which lent itself perfectly to crafting spells and incantations.

"What kind of spell? I'm not sure we have enough power between the two of us to kill all three harpies."

The more witches reciting a spell, the more powerful its effects were.

Kathy shook her head. "I wasn't thinking about killing them. They're mythical creatures. Killing them could disturb the balance and create a whole mess that we don't want to have to deal with."

"Then what are you thinking?"

"Banishing them back to hell."

"Wouldn't that just delay them until they find away around the spell and get Mark anyway?" Samantha asked.

"Well, if we don't know about it…"

"Kathy, as much as I want him to pay for what he's done, we have to protect him."

"I know, I know." She let out a frustrated breath and went on, "If I word the spell correctly, the banishment will keep the harpies away indefinitely."

"Do you think you can come up with a spell that can do that?"

Kathy smirked. "Between the two of us, I'm the better

HARPY

option for spell crafting."

Samantha excelled at potion making, which was obvious from the effects it had on the harpy tied up in their dining room.

"Okay," the older sister said. "You get started on that. I'm going to try to get some answers out of our harpy friend."

"Be careful."

"Of course."

While Kathy escaped to the kitchen to grab a pad of paper and a pen and start crafting the spell, Samantha stepped toward the harpy tied up to the dining room chair. It had been scratched and nicked in the attack, and further pushed to the limits by the creature struggling against her restraints.

The harpy glared at the witch as she approached.

"I was hoping we'd be able to talk." Samantha grabbed a nearby chair and took a seat a careful distance away from the harpy. "You can talk, right?"

The harpy hissed at Samantha. "Yes, I can talk."

"Good. Why don't we start with names? I'm Samantha."

Glaring at her with beady eyes, the harpy refused to answer.

"You must not be accustomed to some of the social etiquette," Samantha said with a grin. "When someone tells you their name, typically you respond with yours. I'm Samantha and *you are*…?" She pushed her persuasion power toward the creature.

"Wren."

The witch nodded. "How fitting. Has that always been your name?"

"I had another name before I became this," Wren said.

"And that would be…?"

"What do you want from me?"

"What I want is to know what *you* want with Mark," Samantha said. "We saw what you did to Jeffrey Jackson, I watched what you did to that girl on East 2nd Street earlier today. My guess is you're not carrying them off to bake cupcakes, so what's your deal?"

"They weren't our original prey," Wren said. "You prevented us from obtaining our target and we had to make…adjustments."

"Your original target being Mark Gad."

Wren nodded, ever so slowly.

"What I don't understand is why you're after him at all," Samantha said. She decided to downplay all of Mark's discretions to get real answers out of Wren. "He was just here telling us what happened between him and Linda. Sure, it's creepy and wrong and immoral, but does it really justify an eternity in hell? I mean, all he did was break a girl's heart, which, yes, led to her taking her life, but I can't imagine that was his goal."

Wren threw her head back and laughed. "You think all of this is over a broken heart? You're fools if you believed a *man's* explanation."

Harpy

"I take it you've had some bad experiences with men?"

"How do you think I became a harpy? Being subjected to ruthless torment at the hands of my husband turned my heart cold—and turned me into a creature who delivers sinners to their ultimate punishment. Just as I did my husband all those years ago."

That explained the evolution of harpies and confirmed what their purpose was.

"Well, I'm sorry you had to go through that—"

"Don't *pity* me," the harpy spat. "What happened to me made me who I am today. And now I live to make people pay for their sins."

"And I'm here to protect them," Samantha said. "So here we are. A stalemate. What I don't understand is that you're different. You have abilities the other two harpies don't. You can control the wind."

Wren smirked. "And?"

"And it's something I've never seen a harpy do before."

"I was a witch before I was a harpy."

"A witch? I didn't realize witches could become harpies."

"Anyone can have their heart turn cold," Wren said. "Anyone can become a harpy."

"So that's it, then?" Samantha sat back in her chair and crossed her legs. "You're a witch who became a harpy and maintained your witch powers while developing some others on your own? Oh, and you want Mark to pay for being a not-great guy." Again, she downplayed what Mark had done. "I don't know, I feel like you've tortured him enough as it is. He's going to have nightmares for years about this. Certainly won't forget what he did. I think you and your other harpy friends can fly off back home."

"You think this is over?"

"I assure you, I do not," Samantha corrected. "Not when two of your harpy friends are still out there looking for the man that my sister and I are trying to protect. Now tell me, what do you think Mark did to make him your next target? Does it have anything to do with Linda? Apparently it has nothing to do with their break-up."

"He didn't just break her heart," Wren nearly shouted. "He crushed her spirit!"

Samantha crossed her arms. She hated pretending to side with Mark, but her strategy seemed to be working. "Still not seeing it. Linda was already depressed before she met Mark. I don't see how him breaking up with her—and visiting her afterward to check in on her—is what led her to kill herself."

"*Visiting* her? During one of his *visits*, he wanted to be with her just one more time. She told him no, but he didn't listen and forced himself on her. *That's* why he didn't want her talking to his wife or her parents or anyone else. He wanted to hide what he'd done to her."

Samantha's blood had run cold and she knew it showed on her face. Inside, she kicked herself for believing Mark's version

HARPY

of the story. She hated that they had to protect a man who was so horrible.

She looked up and tried to find the words to cover her surprise, but there wasn't any way to hide it.

Kathy peeked her head out from around the door to the kitchen and waved her sister toward her. Ordinarily, Samantha would be upset by the interruption, but it gave her the perfect excuse to leave the room.

"Just a minute," she told Wren and crossed the room to Kathy. "What is it?"

Kathy handed her a piece of paper they usually wrote their shopping list on. "What do you think?"

Samantha read the spell over. "It might work."

"Did you get anything out of the harpy?"

"Her name's Wren. She used to be a witch."

"I didn't realize that was possible."

"Me neither," Samantha said. "Makes me wonder if she's part of something bigger."

"Bigger?"

"More than just the harpies," Samantha explained. "Like a coven or a supergroup or something."

"I don't think she's a part of New Kids on the Block or anything like that," Kathy said. "Harpies become harpies because they've been wrong somehow."

"Their hearts turn cold," Samantha corrected.

"Okay, so if she was a witch before, that doesn't

automatically protect her heart. You and I can both vouch for that."

"Yeah," Samantha said, not convinced. She didn't like the idea that Wren had been a witch before and she feared there was more to it.

"I just want to get the harpies away from Mark and forget that we ever helped him," Kathy said. "What else did you find out from her?"

"That there's more to Mark's story."

Kathy scoffed. "Of course there is."

"Not only was he harassing Linda, he raped her."

Kathy's eyes grew wide. "You're kidding."

"Nobody would joke about that."

Sighing, Kathy said, "And we still need to protect him! I hate this."

"From the harpies, yes. But maybe we could find evidence to support the counter-suit Linda's parents filed against Mark."

"Do you think evidence like that exists?" Kathy asked. "Unless they were caught on camera or something, we've got nothing. It's a he-said, she-said."

"I know. We'll have to think about that. First we need to save him from Wren and her pack. Let's go see if she has any other revelations."

Turning back into the dining room, Samantha's heart stopped when she saw that Wren's chair was empty. The ropes holding her had been frayed through, likely from the harpy's claws. At the front of the house, the door sat wide open.

"Where'd she go?" Kathy asked.

"She ran off."

"Damn it. What do we do now?"

"Find Mark and get him to confess," Samantha said. "I'm tired of being in the middle of this. We'll get his confession on tape and give him the ultimatum: get carted away by the harpies or go to prison."

CHAPTER 33

Mark bolted out of the sisters' house and zig-zagged through the streets of the neighborhood. Sunnydale Boulevard, Hilltop Drive, Highview Boulevard, back to Arlington Road, then finally turning onto Upland Drive. He hoped to get those creatures to lose his trail. His heart was pounding and sweat dripped down his face, but still he pressed on. It was either that or die.

At least that's what he was afraid of.

As he passed West Grandview Boulevard, he saw a shadow forming on the street beside him. Chancing a look over his shoulder, he saw two of those bird creatures following him.

Mark ran over to the sidewalk, which was tucked under tree canopy. He nearly tripped once on the uneven slabs, but he regained his footing quickly and pressed on. His sides ached with cramps and he was gasping for breath—he probably needed to cut back on the cigarettes—but that didn't stop him. He couldn't stop.

The sidewalk ended abruptly, giving way to the open front yard of the neighboring houses and suddenly he was maneuvering around decorative light posts, flagpoles, flower gardens, and even a parked car at the end of the driveway.

Hearing the screech of the bird creatures above him, he decided he was wasting more time than he was distracting them, so he darted back out onto the street and continued on to where Upland ended at Glenwood Boulevard, which was adorned with trees in the center parkway.

Thinking he'd be able to hook around and keep under the cover of trees until he got to a public building he could escape into, he made to turn left onto the quiet street, only to stop short as a car came passing by.

He felt the rush of air as one of the bird creatures lunged down at him, and he darted quickly across the street into an open field.

Jumping over a short row of bushes, Mark realized he had run right into the middle of a golf course. But he didn't care. He was running for his life. With any luck, a stray golf ball would knock one of the creatures out and then that'd at least *help* with his current problem. Maybe he could even fight off the creature until help came.

Mark found a small patch of trees and slowed to catch his ragged breath. He wasn't in shape, no matter how he looked at it. Surely, those creatures wouldn't be able to see him under the trees. Leaning against the trunk of a maple, he allowed himself two minutes to breathe some fresh air into his smoker's lungs before he moved on.

But the screech above him proved sinister as the creatures dove through the branches of the maple right toward him. With the snapping of twigs and branches above him, he darted out from under the cover of the tree and ran across the next fairway toward the fence, hoping to jump over it. He didn't know what was on the other side, but it had to be better than this open course.

Before he made it to the fence, though, he felt the cold talons of one of the bird creatures wrap around his arm. His body collided with the grassy lawn. Seconds later, the other creature was there, pressing his other arm to the ground.

Mark struggled, trying to break free, but their hold was too strong.

He was pinned.

CHAPTER 34

Samantha set the bowl of water on the floor in the foyer. She positioned the bowl so their makeshift altar was right over top of a blood smear leftover from the attack.

Kathy stepped down the stairs with four yellow candles pressed against her chest by her arms. Yellow represented clarity, which is what they needed in order to find Mark Gad. "How can we even be sure that blood is Mark's?"

"We can't." Samantha took the candles from her sister and laid them out to the north, south, east, and west. "But we know it's not from either of us and it wasn't here before the attack, so it has to be either Mark's or from one of the harpies. Locating any of them will still tell us what we want to know."

Location rituals required something belonging to the

person they were trying to locate. What could be more personal than blood?

Kathy lit a match and held it at the wick of each candle. "You have the spell?"

Samantha set *The Art of Magic* on the floor beside the altar. "Right here."

"Ready?"

"I'm ready to get *all* of this over with."

"You and me both."

The sisters sat across from each other and held hands over the altar. They turned to the book and recited the location ritual spell:

> *I call on the strength of my power,*
> *Show Mark's face in the water.*

They repeated the spell two more times, allowing the magic to flow through them and show Mark's location in the water. Both sisters were silent, waiting for his image to appear in the bowl. It was important to create a sense of calm and tranquility to focus on the magic.

The gong of the doorbell cut through the silence, making both sisters jump and pull away.

"Who is that?" Samantha asked.

Kathy, who was closest to the door, stood and said, "I'll get rid of them."

HARPY

Since they made their altar so close to the front door, she could only open it slightly and squeeze her way through. She didn't want to disturb the candles and interrupt the ritual—if it hadn't already been interrupted by the doorbell.

Waiting just outside, Jeremy gave Kathy a very confused look as she squeezed through the door.

"What are you doing?" he asked.

Kathy closed the door behind her and threw her thumb back to the door. "Oh, um…Samantha is cleaning the floors and I didn't want to accidentally sweep in any dust. What's up?"

"I was hoping I could come in and we could talk," he said. "Could we go around back or something?" He pointed up the driveway.

"No," Kathy said quickly. The house was a mess from the attack and they didn't have time to talk, even though she knew they needed to. She took a seat on the steps, which gave them a few feet buffer between them and the door. "Sit. Let's talk out here."

He let out a heavy sigh and sat beside her, leaning forward on his knees and staring at his hands. "I can't stand it that you're mad at me. And you were right, earlier, that I was ignoring you. I didn't realize it until you pointed it out, but I should've. I'm sorry."

She nodded, her mind still on the attack and finding Mark and the revelation of what he did. The tables had turned and now she was the one not giving Jeremy her full attention. But she needed to get rid of him so she and Samantha could get to Mark before Talon and the rest of the harpies.

"Apology accepted." Kathy patted his knee and stood, hoping he'd follow suit and leave.

"Wait, really?" He looked confused. Worse, he looked suspicious.

She shrugged. "Sure. We had a fight, you apologized, I accepted. It's the way things go with us." The cycle they just kept repeating.

He stood and held her hands. "Well, I still want to make it up to you."

"Jeremy, it's fine," she said. "We'll talk more later. Samantha is going to get mad at me if I don't get back in there and help her." She gave him a quick kiss and tried to head back inside, but he held on to her.

"Wait a minute," he insisted. "I planned a weekend trip. Just the two of us. I booked a cabin in the Allegheny Forest. Secluded, no one around us, no responsibilities." He moved in closer and hugged her, kissing her cheek as he did. "No interruptions…"

"This weekend?" Would they still be chasing harpies by the weekend?

"Yeah, I figured we'd leave tomorrow."

"Tomorrow! Oh."

He pulled away. "You don't sound excited."

She looked up into his disappointed eyes and couldn't stand

to know that she was the cause of it. "No, it's not that. It's just—unexpected."

Jeremy's face lit up again. "I wanted it to be a surprise. Michael had mentioned that his family owned a cabin out there and I thought it'd be a good getaway for the two of us. We'll leave when I get out of class tomorrow and come back Sunday."

She smiled at him. "Okay, sure. I guess I'll see you tomorrow then."

"Yes!" He shook his fist in celebration. "I love you, Kathy."

Before she could say it back to him, he had pulled her in for another kiss. The kind they hadn't really shared in a while. She forgot where she was and who could be watching. All that mattered was her and Jeremy. Together.

When he finally pulled away, Kathy tried to hide the fact that she needed to catch her breath. The smile spread across her face gave it away, though. Jeremy returned the smile and raised his eyebrows as if to ask if she wanted to continue.

She swallowed hard and nodded to the door. "I should get back inside. I'll see you tomorrow."

He watched her walk up the steps and took a few steps backward toward his car on the street. "Be ready by three!"

Kathy waved and then escaped inside to a whole different world. Jeremy had made her forget about the mess in the house and the ritual they were doing, but it all came back to her as soon as she stepped inside.

"What's at three?" Samantha set the candles on the dining

room table. The bowl had already been returned to the kitchen.

"Jeremy planned a weekend trip for us. We're leaving tomorrow."

"We have some things to do before either of us can enjoy our weekend—if we're even able to," Samantha said.

Kathy's shoulders dropped. "Yeah. Did you find Mark?"

Samantha held up her car keys. "Yep, we need to go. I grabbed a few pre-made potions, the spell you wrote for the harpies, and a weapon, just in case. I want to be prepared."

They stepped outside and walked to the car.

"Is he close by?" Kathy asked.

"Not far. Two of the harpies are circling overtop Mark, keeping an eye on him." Samantha got in the car and started it. "They're probably waiting for Wren, who is still under the effects of my potion and can't fly."

"Well, at least there's that." Kathy held on to the handles as her sister barreled out of the driveway and gunned it down the street. "It's a good thing they travel in packs."

"For now," Samantha said. "Let's just hope the potion doesn't wear off and then we have three pissed off, full-strength harpies to fight off in plain daylight."

CHAPTER 35

here!" Samantha threw the car in park, turned on her four-way lights—there really wasn't any room to park on Cherry Street, which the honking oncoming traffic reminded her—and followed her sister out toward the middle of the J.C. Martin Golf Course.

"Hey! We're in the middle of a game here!" one of the golfers yelled to them as they raced through the course. Two other men in khaki pants and polo shirts tucked around their bellies stared at them dumbfounded.

Being that it was four o'clock on a Thursday, there were only a few golfers out on the course. The after work crew had yet to arrive in full force for their afternoon outing. That turned out to be a blessing as Samantha and Kathy raced toward Mark Gad and the harpies along the fairway on the first hole, luckily shaded by enough trees to keep them hidden. At the edge of the course, there was a chain-link fence with overgrown foliage that marked the dividing line with the Erie Zoo. Fitting for the creatures they were chasing down.

As the sisters rushed forward, they spotted Mark. He lay on his back near the fence, his shoulders pinned down by two of the harpies. In the air, Wren struggled to stay afloat, flapping her wings and trying desperately to catch a drift.

As they got closer, so did Wren, who seemed to finally get her bearings and tucked her wings against her body as she dove straight toward Mark.

Kathy broke into a sprint to get closer in range, raised her hands, and froze the attack. Wren floated magically in place only a few feet from Mark with her claws extended for the attack. The other two harpies held Mark in place and looked up at their third charging toward him. Meanwhile, Mark looked terrified at the oncoming attack.

Kathy's magic allowed the sisters to gain better control of the situation.

Samantha charged one of the harpies pinning Mark. Raising up the dagger that she brought with her, she sliced at the back of the harpy right between her wings. The impact made the harpy break away from Kathy's magic and let out a screech.

Before Samantha had time to strike again, the harpy pinned her to the ground and fought to slash the witch's throat.

HARPY

Running to her sister's aid, Kathy kicked at the harpy and managed to get the creature off of Samantha, who jumped to her feet.

"Are you okay?" Kathy asked quickly.

Samantha nodded and then turned as she noticed the rest of the scene had unfroze as well. Luckily, since they had managed to free Mark of one harpy, he was able to move out of the way in time to evade Wren's airborne attack.

Kathy extended her hand to the injured harpy and froze her again. "We each take one?"

Samantha nodded and raced toward Wren, brandishing her knife. Kathy charged toward the harpy trying to pin Mark to the ground once more.

Wren swatted and kicked at Samantha, delivering deep scrapes and cuts along her forearms.

As Samantha fought and her heart beat faster, her clothes became smeared with her own blood. Still, she was able to fend off the harpy's attack, managing to secure a few of her own jabs at the creature as well.

Meanwhile, Kathy kicked the harpy she faced away from Mark. He turned to run away, but the witch grabbed his arm and put him behind her, against the fence.

"You're not going anywhere!" she told him.

At least putting him behind her created a safe buffer between him and the harpy.

The harpy swatted and screeched, but Kathy mostly

managed to keep her distance and avoid the creature's attacks. The only time she faulted was when she heard Mark bump against the chain-link fence.

She tried to catch a quick glance to make sure he wasn't running away and felt the claws of the harpy tear into the flesh of her bicep.

Angry, Kathy drove her foot against the harpy's stomach, sending her flopping back on the ground beside the still-frozen harpy they fought off earlier.

Kathy snatched up Mark's arm and bellowed at him, "Stay here!"

Seeing that her sister was hurt and that the other two harpies had grouped together, Samantha took a more offensive approach to her attack, driving Wren back toward the other two harpies. With a swift kick, she knocked Wren to the ground and quickly retreated to her sister.

Kathy put up her hands and froze all of the harpies as Samantha dug out the spell Kathy had written.

"Hopefully this works," the older sister said.

> *Guiding spirits, we call to thee.*
> *Rid these creatures, hear our plea.*
> *Erase their charge, let him be.*
> *Banish them for eternity!*

Instantly, dark clouds rolled in above them, disturbing the

HARPY

clear blue skies and sending an instant chill to the balmy summer air. A streak of lightning struck down from the clouds to where the harpies stood, striking them with a flash of light. In an instant, all three of them were gone. All that was left was a small hole where the lightning had hit the ground.

"Is that it?" Samantha asked.

Kathy looked up as the dark clouds slowly rolled away. "I think so."

"That was—you're bleeding!" Samantha grabbed Kathy's hand and examined her arms.

"So are you!"

"We need to get this taken care of," Samantha said. "We don't know what kind of infections those things had."

Kathy looked around. "I want to get out of here too."

"Is it over?" Mark asked as they turned back to him.

The sisters paused when they saw him. Then Samantha stepped toward him and grabbed his arm above his elbow, pulling him toward a tree away from the mark their spell had left behind.

Under the cover of the leaves, Samantha pushed Mark against the trunk of the tree and jabbed her finger into his chest. "You *lied* to us!"

"I told you everything!" he pleaded.

"No, you didn't," Kathy said.

"You raped her."

Mark stammered. "How would you—who told you that?"

"The harpies told us," Samantha said. "And they wouldn't lie about that. It's the reason they were after you. You didn't just break her heart and cheat on your wife, you took advantage of that girl and used her."

He put up a finger. "Hey, I cared for her."

Samantha snatched his finger and bent it back. "If you cared for her at all, you wouldn't have done that to her!"

He winced until she let go.

"So what are we going to do with you, Mark?" Kathy asked. "We took care of the harpies for you, but we still don't like you at all."

"You're a pervert and you're dangerous and you deserved what the harpies were going to give you," Samantha added.

"The problem is, before you spend an eternity in hell, we want to make sure you experience hell on earth too," Kathy said.

"What?" Mark looked between the sisters. "What are you talking about?"

"You're going to confess to raping her," Samantha said.

"You're going to give that girl's parents some closure," Kathy added. "By serving time for what you took from them."

"But that's not—there aren't any charges against me," he said. "You can't do that!"

Samantha motioned to the lightning mark on the ground. "I think we just proved to you that we can do anything."

"But—but—"

"Would you like us to call the harpies back here to escort

you to eternal damnation?" Kathy asked. She had no idea if she could, but he didn't know that.

Mark looked at her with wide eyes. "You wouldn't."

She stepped forward, the image of Debra during her recounting of her daughter's torment playing in her mind. "Try me."

He breathed in a shuddering breath. "Okay. I'll do what you say."

"You'll confess?" Samantha pushed.

He nodded. "Yes, I'll confess."

"To everything?" Kathy said. "Samantha can come up with some truth potions to give you, just to make sure you keep your word."

"No!" he cried. "None of that. I'll say it all myself."

"Good." Kathy turned to Samantha, unsure of how she should feel. They stopped the harpies, protected their victim, but it still didn't feel right. It didn't make things better for Linda Powers' parents.

No amount of magic could bring their daughter back.

CHAPTER 36

athy had several piles of clothes spread across her bed. Her empty suitcase sat on a chair beside her dresser. She had no idea what kind of things she and Jeremy were going to be doing on this weekend adventure—although she could think of one thing in particular. But the rest of it made it hard to pack.

Rubbing at the bandage on her arm—the results of yesterday's harpy attack, the wounds of which had already started itching—she set aside her swimsuit. Swimming in a pond—or even a public pool—with an open wound was a sure way to get an infection.

"Are you taking all of that?" Samantha peeked her head in the door. She had her own set of bandages—worse than Kathy.

"I'm deciding."

HARPY

"Kathy, you're going for a weekend, not a month." She stepped in and took a seat on the edge of the bed. A stack of clothes threatened to topple over. "Are you even going to be wearing much?"

Kathy took the stack and added it to her suitcase. "Ha ha. We do more than that."

"I guess I'm just surprised you're even still going."

"Why?"

Samantha shrugged. "Did he ever really apologize for ignoring you?"

"Yes, he did yesterday," Kathy said smugly. "Right before we chased after the harpies and got Mark to confess."

Mark Gad, who had actually confessed and was now at the Erie Police Department—hopefully even sitting in a jail cell until his sentencing.

"I'm just saying, isn't this his usual thing?" Samantha asked. "Do something wrong again and again until you finally decide to take a stand and he makes up for it by a big romantic gesture without actually changing his behavior."

Kathy grabbed a pair of pants and folded them as a distraction to keep from meeting her sister's eyes. As she tucked the jeans in her suitcase, she shrugged. "No relationship is perfect. I love him, flaws and all."

Samantha took a deep breath. "Okay. I just want you to be aware of these patterns. I don't want you to get hurt."

"I know."

"Well, I have a lunch date with Steven." Samantha stood and straightened some of the clothes on the bed. "If I don't see you, have a great time this weekend."

Kathy came around the bed and gave her sister a hug. "How are you going to explain the bandages?"

Samantha pulled away and looked at her arms. "First of all, I'll wear sleeves. And second, I'll probably tell him it was an allergic reaction to something—or something like that."

"I'm just saying, isn't that your usual thing? Lying to him again and again until he gets mad enough to take a stand and you try to make up for it with a big romantic gesture without actually changing your habitual lying."

Samantha rolled her eyes. "Yeah, yeah. I get it, but this is different. I have a reason to lie."

"And Jeremy has a lot on his plate."

She chewed on the inside of her cheek and pursed her lips. "Touché, little sister."

"Have fun on your date!"

CHAPTER 37

I want to apologize for being so weird these last few days."
Samantha set her glass of wine down.

Steven had surprised her by taking her to a bar, not far from
where she and Kathy had first spotted the harpies. It was a classy
place, modeled as a speakeasy with dim lighting, valvet window
treatments, and leather seating.

"Honey, you're always weird," he said with a smirk.

"Not true!"

"You're the only soon-to-be-twenty-two-year-old I know
who has a Roth IRA. And I work in finance, so I would know."

"I just like to be prepared."

"I'm just saying, you have quirks."

"Says the one who likes to pretend he's swanky with a trip to a make-believe speakeasy." When Samantha heard the words out loud, she thought they sounded too angry, so she added, "Sorry. I do like this place."

He smiled. "I do too. I also like that it's pretty quiet."

Samantha looked around. There were maybe two or three other tables that had people. The bar seemed more like a dinner and an evening crowd, not so much a lunch crowd.

"I hope that this makes up for our failed date the other day—and the failed make-up date," she said.

"To be fair, I'm the one who asked *you* to lunch," he said. "So technically this is my date. You still owe me those do-overs."

She smiled at him. "Well, Kathy's away for the weekend, so I think that can be arranged."

"No last-minute interruptions?"

"I'm free until Monday," she said. Preparing for her first day at a real job would take the better part of Sunday. As she said, she liked to be prepared. They both knew that her weekend wasn't completely open but she didn't want to bring it up at the moment.

"Good. I want you all to myself."

"Be careful what you wish for."

He grinned. "You know, the other day when you were at my apartment, I wasn't even paying attention to anything except you. But then you dashed out of there like a bat out of hell."

Samantha looked down, feeling guilty that she had completely ditched Steven like that. Worse, that he remembered it and was bringing it up.

"But when I chased after you and I saw that you ran out to save that girl, I saw a side of you I didn't know about before," he went on. "Someone who would put herself out there to help other people."

"Steven, I'm sorry for running out like that—"

He put up his hand to stop her. "I admired that about you. That you care about other people. Strangers, even. And when you saw that you didn't make it in time and you started crying…I loved you even more, which I didn't think was possible."

She offered him a sad smile, not sure what else to do. She felt awkward being complimented for what she viewed as one of her biggest failures.

"And with the way you're always helping your sister—even if I do find it annoying sometimes—I love that about you too. I realize that I never want to let someone so selfless slip through my fingers and out of my life."

Samantha's heart started beating faster as she suspected what was coming next. When Steven got down on one knee, he confirmed her thoughts.

He pulled out a black box that was almost impossible to see in the dark lighting. "Samantha Walker, will you marry me?"

She stared at him, completely surprised. Finally, she held either side of his face and kissed him. "Yes, I will!"

SIREN

COVEN: BOOK 2

Sometimes betrayal is just one small act...

DAVID NETH

While scouting possible wedding locations on Presque Isle, Samantha and Kathy cast a spell to prevent a man from driving his boat right onto shore. Shrugging it off as a close call, the sisters return their focus to their lives: Samantha's upcoming wedding, and Kathy's struggling personal and professional life.

However, their little diversion spell ignites the fury of Heather, a siren who lives to sway men in loving relationships into a fiery betrayal that results in their death. She turns her attention to the men in the witches' lives as payback for foiling her plan on Presque Isle. After several close calls, Samantha and Kathy force their boyfriends to coexist in one house so they can protect them, but the siren's attacks keep hitting closer to home.

With tensions rising in the overcrowded house and everyone almost at their breaking point, the witches must find a way to stop Heather before she can succeed in her mission to kill their men.

Siren is the second book in the Coven series, which serves as a prequel series to the Under the Moon series.

SIREN

COVEN: BOOK 2

Read on for an excerpt of the second book
in the Coven series!

DAVID NETH

CHAPTER 1

- JULY 1988 -

The truck rocked back and forth as Justin pulled onto the rough gravel parking lot of the Presque Isle Marina. Beside him, his girlfriend Nancy clung to the handle above the door as they maneuvered over the potholes before coming to a resting spot where Justin put the truck in park.

"All right, here we go," he said. "You ready?"

She smiled at him. "I'm going to put on some sun lotion. You should too."

"I will," he promised. "But first I need to run to the locker room and change into my trunks."

"You didn't put them on before you left the house?" she asked, still with a smile.

"Sorry," he said. "Was in too much of a rush to see you." *And*

SIREN

Sandy wouldn't have bought my story that I was going in to work today if I left dressed for a day at the beach.

Justin crossed the parking lot with his backpack slung over his shoulder and went to the locker room. Inside, he began to undress but stopped when he noticed his wedding ring still resting on his finger.

His heart began racing and he quickly replayed every moment he and Nancy had since he picked her up. She hadn't given any indication that she noticed the ring. And it was his left hand, and she was sitting to his right.

With some force and a good measure of twisting and turning, he pulled the ring off and slipped it in the side pocket of his backpack, zipping it back up for safe keeping. It would need to go back on before he went home to Sandy.

Back outside, Justin tossed his bag in the back of the truck cab and absently rubbed his bare finger.

"What's the matter?" Nancy asked.

"Nothing," he said quickly. "You ready?"

"Don't you need to put lotion on?"

He smirked. "Bring it. You can rub me down when we're on the water."

She laughed and rolled her eyes, but slipped the lotion in her bag.

Together, they walked out on the dock and Justin stepped onto the boat. The *Thunderbird* was his grandfather's, but it was left to Justin after he passed. He made an effort to get out on it as much as he could—twice as much if he counted his outings with Nancy too.

Justin extended his hand and helped Nancy onto the boat. They'd both been on enough times that they fell into an easy routine of disengaging from the dock, starting the engine, and slowly backing out into the water.

When they emerged into Presque Isle Bay and were far enough away from the shore and other boaters, Justin kicked up the throttle and drove out toward the Erie Harbor Channel that led to the rest of Lake Erie. Every time he took Nancy out in public he was always careful to make sure that nobody spotted them.

Not that the *Thunderbird* was a unique boat or anything.

Once they got through the channel, Justin slowed the engine. Nancy tapped him on the bare shoulder.

"Put something on before you burn," she said. "Do you want me to do it?"

"Sure." Behind his sunglasses, Justin's eyes darted back and forth to the other boats and scanned along shore too. He liked to think he was just being careful, but he knew he was really just being paranoid.

Behind him, Nancy rubbed the lotion on his shoulders, along his arms, and down his back. He obliged as much as he could while still keeping the boat in motion.

Nancy leaned over and said into his ear over the roar of the passing wind, "What's your rush?"

SIREN

"Want to make sure we get a good spot." Justin steered the boat around Gull Point and toward the west side of Presque Isle. There would be fewer eyes there and fewer chances of being caught.

His heart hadn't stopped racing since he took off his wedding ring.

He finally slowed the boat as they approached Budny Beach along the western shore of Presque Isle. Slowing to a crawl, he pulled in as close as he dared to the shore without getting in the way of anyone else. It would be easier to swim in shallower water. And if they were swimming, there would be less of a chance of someone spotting him.

Nancy pulled off her T-shirt once Justin cut the engine and stood in a tiny pink bikini.

"Oh wow," he said.

She smiled and turned for him, modeling. "Oh, this old thing?" She laughed and stepped to the back of the boat. "Come on, let's get in the water!"

Justin tossed his sunglasses on the seat and jumped off the side of the boat. When the cold water hit him, he finally felt his heart rate begin to return to normal. He and Nancy splashed each other—he even tried to carry her over his shoulder, but the sandy floor was just a little too deep for him to maintain his footing.

When they got tired, they both crawled back onto the boat and lay in the sun, fully embracing the heat that had been plaguing Erie for over a month now.

"Did you pack any snacks in that bag of tricks of yours?" Justin asked.

Nancy sat up and made a face. "I think so, but let me check." She got up and bent over her bag to inspect, pulling out a towel, the sunscreen, and a couple bottles of water and piling them on the seat.

Justin came up and wrapped his arms around her from behind, planting kisses along her shoulder.

She laughed. "Babe, not here."

He pulled away and leaned on the edge of the driver's seat. "But you look so—"

"Shoot!"

"What is it?"

"I know I packed some granola bars, but I must've left them in my other bag," she said. "Back in the truck. They're probably all melted!"

Justin shrugged. "So what? They're wrapped."

"Yeah," she said with a sigh, then patted her stomach. "I'm just getting kind of hungry."

"Me too," he admitted. He hoped to be able to stay out on the lake all day. Another trip back to the marina would mean more opportunity for them to be seen. But baking in the sun all day without any food didn't add up to anything good.

"Do you mind if we go back?" Nancy asked. She looked around and added, "There aren't too many boats out here.

Maybe we can get a good spot when we come back."

Justin looked toward the shore, then down at Nancy's pleading eyes. "Yeah, I suppose that's okay."

She kissed him. "Thanks babe! Can't wait to get back out here and spend more time with you!"

He couldn't keep the smile off his face as he started the boat back up and slowly backed away from the swimming area. When he was clear away, he kicked it into high gear, glancing over at Nancy as her long, wet hair blew in the wind.

As he rounded Gull Point and sped back across Thompson Bay, his ears tuned in to something that sounded absolutely beautiful. A woman's voice, singing. Somewhere along the shore. It was mesmerizing.

Who was it?

The song sounded familiar yet entirely new, all at the same time. It was almost…magical, the way it took him out of himself. He felt as if he was floating above himself and watching as he directed the boat toward the shore. As Nancy stared at him with panic. How she tried to pull him away.

All the while, the beautiful voice sang the song that completely took him in its grasp.

CHAPTER 2

S o, what do you think?" Cheryl Anderson extended her arms out to showcase the location she picked out. Her salon-created blonde hair fluttered in the breeze.

Samantha stepped further onto the grass with Steven and Kathy trailing behind. "It's nice."

"Nice?" Kathy said. "Sam, this is gorgeous!"

They were on Presque Isle scouting possible wedding locations. For the ceremony, at least. Samantha was insistent on having a wedding on the water. She could picture the wedding photos in her head and she intended to make that vision a reality.

"Look, you can set up an archway here and get married with the city in the background." Cheryl moved to a spot near the water. "Or, you can shift it over there and have a more lush, green backdrop."

Samantha glanced over at her green option. It was another picnic area with a pull-off from the road that served as a makeshift parking lot. It was just like the one they stood on, where families could picnic and fish and spend a weekend. Just as she and Kathy had done when they were younger.

"Yeah…"

Steven hooked his arm around her waist. "You don't seem sure."

Cheryl stepped closer and continued to sell the location. "There's plenty of parking for guests. It's not too far into the park where people could get lost. I think this is a fantastic option."

Samantha bit her lip and looked around. The area was beautiful, but it was also littered with geese poop, interrupted by passing cars, and had the audience of other picnickers. Would they be able to have a sense of privacy on their wedding day?

Just as the thought came to her, a motor boat loudly came around the bend from the Presque Isle Marina from the other side of the peninsula. Nope. No privacy, whatsoever.

"Maybe we should keep looking," Samantha finally said.

Cheryl let out a heavy sigh, mourning her "perfect" suggestion. By time they all piled back in the car and she was behind the wheel directing them back toward the rest of the park, Cheryl seemed to forget all about her first suggestion.

"Oh, this next one is just breathtaking," she said as she navigated the winding roads through the marshy peninsula. The open windows made it hard to hear her, but the July breeze wafting off the lake felt nice in the sunshine.

As they passed another pull-off, Cheryl waved at it. "That over there looks out across the water to where we just were. You were right to turn it down, Samantha, you wouldn't have been able to enjoy your special day without an audience from a bunch of strangers. Nope, your wedding should include only the people you invite."

Samantha looked out the window and watched as the road weaved through the park with paved bike paths and other picnic areas. For one stretch, they had a beautiful view of the city across the bay.

"This is gorgeous," Kathy said from the backseat.

Samantha nodded. Something was off with her today. She was excited to start wedding planning, but today she was just not in the mood to fill up her day with to-dos. She wanted to be able to enjoy the sunshine, like everyone else in Presque Isle seemed to be doing. Scouting for wedding locations seemed like a chore.

Cheryl pulled into a parking lot at the bend of another curve. "Now, this one is another excellent option." She parked the car and went to turn it off before she caught the look on Samantha's face. "What's the matter?"

SIREN

Samantha shook her head as she looked around. At the pavilion just off the parking lot, the boat advertising tours of the bay docked nearby, and the number of people swarming along the sidewalk leading to the Perry Monument. "Not here. This isn't the right place."

"Why don't we just get out and look?" Steven suggested.

"Yeah, there are a lot of amenities here. Plenty of parking for guests, bathrooms, beautiful views."

"Beautiful views?" Samantha blurted. "Isn't that a smokestack I see over there?"

"Well, there are plenty of other views to see from out there," Cheryl countered. "If you want to get out I can show—"

"No, I'd rather just move on to the next place."

"Sam," Kathy said. "You didn't even give this a try."

"Look, Kathy, this isn't where I want to get married," Samantha snapped. "End of discussion. Now, can we please move on?"

Tension-filled silence swept over the car. Kathy glared up at her sister, not liking the person she was becoming as a bride. She looked across to Steven and could tell he had similar thoughts, but he gave a shrug that said, "What are you going to do?"

Cheryl quickly recovered from Samantha's outburst. Likely due to the fact that she was used to working with demanding brides. "Well all right then, on we go!" She put the car in drive and continued up the road through the park.

Not far down the road, Cheryl slowed and pointed. "The Lagoon picnic area is nice, but there's not much of the view you said you wanted. We can take a look, but—"

"That's okay," Samantha said. "What else is there?"

Cheryl pulled back onto the road. "Well, I have a few more options. They'll take bit more work, but it's still manageable."

"This pull-off here has a nice view," Kathy suggested from the backseat. "Doesn't look like there's anyone here, either."

"And how many different camera angles are we going to be able to get from there?" Samantha fired back. "Besides, that's a gravel parking lot. My dress would be ruined."

Kathy bit down on her lips to hold in her retort.

"No, of course you'd want to preserve your dress as best you can," Cheryl said. "So I suppose that rules out a beach wedding?"

Samantha rocked her head back and forth. "I'd be open to that."

"Oh, super!" Cheryl turned off into a parking area that was swarming with cars and people in swimsuits and bags with sand toys.

"This isn't what I was thinking—"

Cheryl held up a finger to Samantha. Kathy and Steven smirked from the back. "Hold on before you start saying no. This place is a little bit off-the-beaten-path, if you will, but it is definitely a contender. Would certainly make for a unique wedding location!"

SIREN

She kept driving away from the parking lot and along Horseshoe Pond with the various houseboats floating on the water. They passed the Coast Guard with the barbed wire chain link fence along the road keeping trespassers out.

"Where are you taking us, Cheryl?" Steven asked.

"Just you wait a see!" she said with a smirk.

Finally, they came to the end of the road and she parked in a small lot along a concrete pier that led to a lighthouse.

"Oh," Samantha said, surprised. Both at the location and the fact that despite a hot July afternoon, there were few people out at this end. She wondered if that was just luck, though.

"Look, there are bathrooms right here," Cheryl pointed out. "Only a few parking spots, so that's something to consider. Maybe you could encourage your guests to carpool, or hire a driver. Maybe a bus or a limo."

"Easy with the expenses, Cheryl," Steven said with a chuckle.

She swatted him playfully. "Come here, you have to see the lighthouse. I thought this would be a beautiful spot for your ceremony. Or at least some pictures." She led them toward the pier as she talked. "Now, this lighthouse is old and a little rusty, but if you put enough distance from it so it's prominent, but the details can't be seen, you'll never even know the difference!"

The trio followed her onto the concrete pier and they started toward the lighthouse.

"Doesn't this pose safety concerns?" Kathy asked.

Cheryl seemed to just notice the water. "Oh yeah, well, maybe. But this view! Oh my gosh, I can't get over it! It's simply gorgeous! Honestly, Samantha, you're going to look stunning standing here in your wedding gown."

Kathy wasn't sure how practical this spot was, but Samantha seemed excited for the first time all day so she didn't burst her sister's bubble just yet. They could have their reality discussion later at home, without the presence of Cheryl egging her on.

Funny how the tables had turned and now Kathy needed to bring her sister back to reality.

Kathy leaned in closer to Steven and muttered, "Perhaps you should see if you can reel in some of Cheryl's suggestions while I try to get a feel for what's going on with your future wife?"

He nodded. "Hey, uh, Cheryl. Can I have a word?"

Kathy nudged her sister's arm as Steven stepped forward to keep walking with Cheryl. The sisters hung back long enough to put some space between them for private conversation.

"So what do you think?" Samantha fussed with her hair being whipped around in the wind. "This is pretty cool, huh?"

"Cool, yes, but not that realistic."

"What do you mean?"

"Samantha, seriously?" Kathy said. "This isn't a wedding venue. It *might* be a place to take pictures, but even that has its challenges. The Coast Guard would never allow a wedding up here."

The hum of a motorboat droned in the distance, growing closer.

"They might make an exception," Samantha said. "With enough...*persuasion*."

"No, you're not using your magic on them and unless you suddenly came into a large sum of money to bribe them or you've thrown away all your morals about selling yourself, then you're fresh out of options."

Samantha shot her sister a look, not appreciating the jab. "What's calling this off is this damn wind." She gathered her hair once again and held it on the side of her neck. "I'm not going to pay a fortune to have my hair done only to have it *un*done in a matter of minutes out here."

The drone of the motorboat got louder as it came into view in Thompson Bay.

"And you were complaining about boats before," Kathy pointed out. "There are boats here too. And could you imagine describing how to get to this place to all of your guests?"

Samantha stared out into the water.

"Are you even listening?" Kathy asked.

"He's going awfully fast."

"Who is? What are you talking about?" Kathy rolled her eyes, frustrated.

Samantha pointed to the motorboat, who was still

zooming full-speed across the bay toward the beach filled with people.

"Yeah." All annoyance evaporated out of Kathy as she noticed the man in the motorboat. "He is going fast. He needs to slow down. The waves from the boat alone could make the swimming hard for the people on the beach." On the boat beside the man was a woman tugging at his arm.

"I'm more concerned about what he's driving toward," Samantha said. "Or rather, *who*. Look." She pointed to a spot along the beach, closer to the pier. A woman stood in a lavender dress with her arm outstretched toward the driver of the boat. She was down the shore away from the swimmers on the beach, making it clear that she was the boat's destination.

"You think he's charging toward her?" Kathy asked.

"Certainly looks that way, doesn't it?" Samantha cast a look in Steven and Cheryl's direction. They were standing at the lighthouse deep in conversation, both facing toward the city, away from the charging motorboat.

"It almost looks like she's drawing him to her."

"Sure," Samantha said dismissively. "We need a spell. Fast."

"Uh, okay, give me a second."

"We don't have a second!"

"You're not helping!" Kathy watched as the boat came closer into view. The driver didn't seem to be aware of his surroundings, only his destination and getting there as quickly as possible. What he needed was a rude awakening and maybe the spray of the lake would do the trick. "Okay, repeat after me."

Together, they recited:

> *Magic spirits,*
> *hear our call:*
> *Raise the water,*
> *build a wall.*
> *Stop this man*
> *from ending it all!*

In a rush, the water from the shore shot up like a geyser, sucking the water from around the bay and spraying it in all directions. The man seemed to regain his rightful mind and eased up on the throttle and quickly tried to steer the boat away from the geyser and the shore. The woman in the boat beside him fell into a nearby seat and held on to the handles with a firm grip.

When the water rained back down, it created a wave that sent water splashing up along the edges of the bay, crashing against the pier and drenching the sisters in the process. The sisters clung to each other as they stumbled back, but managed to keep themselves from falling over the other side of the pier from the force of the wave. With one quick check, Kathy confirmed that nobody else had fallen into the water.

"Looks like it worked." She looked out at the bay. The water was still lapping up against the shore and the swimmers on the beach were all retreating further up the sand.

"Yeah, but now I'm soaked," Samantha complained. "Good thing it's warm today. Too bad it can't get out the stench of algae."

Steven and Cheryl hurried up the pier, both of them wet, though not as bad as the sisters.

"Are you guys okay?" he asked, taking Samantha in his arms.

"Just peachy," she said. "How are you so dry?"

"We hid behind the lighthouse," he said.

"Maybe this isn't such a good spot to have the ceremony," Cheryl said, stating the obvious.

"Let's just get back to the car and go home," Samantha said. "I want to change into dry clothes." She sniffed her arm, then added, "And take a shower."

"Come on, let's go," Cheryl ushered them back to the car. "We'll pick up the venue hunt another day."

Kathy let the rest of them pass by as she took another look out into the bay. Something about the whole situation didn't sit well with her. The man in the boat was completely out of it and the woman with him seemed to be scared. Almost as if he was under a spell. And that woman on the beach—

Kathy nearly stumbled backward when she finally spotted the woman in the lavender dress. She was scowling in Kathy's direction, soaking wet. The way she stared at Kathy made it seem like she knew Kathy was the one who cast the spell that caused the geyser.

Turning, Kathy jogged to catch up to the others, hoping they didn't just gain an enemy they knew nothing about.

CHAPTER 3

H i, what can I get for you?" Kathy asked with a forced smile. "Yeah, can I get a footlong hot dog, a bacon cheeseburger, and some curly fries?" A man asked, looking up at the menu above Kathy's head as he ordered. He had a nasty sunburn. At least, to Kathy it looked like he did. It was hard to tell under the array of neon lights swarming on the ceiling of the fine food establishment she had the displeasure to call "work."

"That'll come with two drinks, is that okay?"

He continued to look up at the menu as he pulled his wallet out of his khaki shorts. "Yeah, that's fine. Just Coke."

Kathy set two empty cups on a tray and nodded to the machines on the other side of the room. "You can fill them over there. Will that be all?"

"Yeah. What's the damage?"

She told him the number and took his money, fishing in the drawer to make change. She handed the coins back to him and piled his order onto the tray as it came out of the kitchen, all the while grateful that the lunch rush seemed to be dying down. Her feet were killing her, but she knew that if she leaned on the counter or looked bored, her manager would yell at her. "If you have time to lean, you have time to clean," was his motto.

"You're all set, sir," she said once the curly fries come up from the kitchen.

"Thanks," the man called over his shoulder as he headed back to his table with his wife and son.

As Kathy watched them her mind went to Samantha. That could be her in a couple years. A wife, a mother. All while Kathy was working checkout in a fast food restaurant at the entry of Presque Isle State Park. When had her life gone off the rails?

"There's my working girl."

Kathy couldn't help but smile when Jeremy leaned across the counter to give her a kiss. He often visited her at work, coming unannounced to see her in action. Always called her his "working girl" too. Although, she suspected he came so often for the curly fries.

"What are you doing here?" she asked, even though she knew the pattern. She was already ringing up his fries and fishing in the tip jar to pay the two dollar charge.

"Just thought I'd surprise you," he said.

"It wasn't at all about the fries, was it?"

He grinned. "Well, if you have any available."

"Curly fries!" someone from the back called.

Kathy reached back and handed them to Jeremy.

"Are you busy?" he asked.

She looked up at the clock. "I could probably take my break. Let me just double check with my manager."

Ten minutes later, they were sitting on the curb at the edge of the parking lot. Jeremy picked at his order of curly fries. Kathy leaned forward and did her best to hide her uniform, all the while wondering how bad she stunk like the fryers.

"You want one?" he offered.

She made a face and shook her head. "I know how that stuff is made. I'm not about to eat any of it."

Jeremy looked down at the carton as if considering if he should continue, then shrugged and reached for another fry. "So how was venue scouting with your sister this morning?"

They had dropped Kathy off at the restaurant on their way out of the park this morning. Lucky for Kathy, the restaurant's stench of the fryers was worse than her lake water shower earlier that morning.

"Meh, not great."

"Samantha didn't find anywhere she liked?"

Kathy rolled her eyes. "She was being so nit-picky. She wants an outdoor wedding, but she doesn't want to deal with other people being around or the wind or the dirty parking lot—but a beach wedding might be an option." She scoffed. "I don't know, she's just driving me nuts with this whole thing."

Jeremy laughed. "She's only been engaged for a few weeks. Why is she even looking for venues now anyway?"

"The sooner they decide on a venue, the sooner they can set the date," Kathy explained. "I guess it all has a domino effect or something."

"Oh."

"Yeah. I don't know. It's like Samantha's become a different person now that she's a *fiancée*." She exaggerated the accent on the word to further mock her sister. "It's like, you're not the first person to get married and you won't be the last. The rest of the world is still turning, so pull your head out of the clouds and pay attention to what's going on around you."

"I'm sorry," Jeremy mused. "Hopefully she'll snap out of it soon."

"I just hope she doesn't become this crazy lady once she's actually married. Or worse, she'll get disappointed because the excitement's over and she's just someone's wife."

"Have you talked to her about this?" Jeremy asked.

"No. She'll get all mad and defensive. I don't know, a part of me just thinks that I need to be patient. It's her wedding day and she has every right to be picky about it."

"Yeah, you'll get to be picky on your wedding day."

Kathy's head picks up. "Should I expect that to come soon?"

He made a face. "No. We're not ready to get married. I'm

still making up classes and you're—"

Jeremy managed to stop himself, but Kathy still understood the implication. The intended end of that sentence: *you're still working low-skilled jobs making virtually nothing.* Yet another reason to be disappointed with herself.

Was that all this was with Samantha? Jealousy that her sister had her life together while Kathy was barely treading water? Kathy would be lying if she said she wasn't at least a little disappointed that she and Jeremy weren't even close to getting married. It didn't even seem like marriage was on Jeremy's mind at all. And he had a point. They *weren't* ready.

"I guess I'm just not really happy with how things are going for me—"

"Oh shoot!" Jeremy said suddenly. "What day is it?"

"Um, Saturday?"

"Monday's the eleventh?"

"I guess so, why?"

"I have a paper due then and I haven't even started it!" He jumped to his feet. "I'm so sorry. I have to get to the library and get started. I'll see you later?"

"Sure." She rose to her feet. "Just call me."

"Okay." He tossed the empty carton in the trash. "It probably won't be until after the paper's done."

Kathy nodded, trying not to look disappointed that their thirty minute date was cut short. Worse, that she was about to pour her heart out to him and he just blew her off.

Siren

He kissed her before walking backward toward his car, his keys jangling in his hand. "Have fun at work!"

She waved him goodbye and watched as he raced off to his car and pulled onto the busy road, back into the city, leaving her stranded in the last place she wanted to be.

To read the rest of **Siren**,
order your copy at
DavidNethBooks.com/Coven

PICK UP THE FIRST BOOK IN THE UNDER THE MOON SERIES!

Kathy and her sister, Samantha, have always been a team.
Throughout their time as witches, they've taken out more than their
share of bad guys. But after Kathy meets Will, who she learns is a
demonic Dark Knight, her loyalties begin to change.

Meanwhile, Samantha doesn't trust Will or his intentions. Still, Kathy
can't help but feel tempted by the dark side as she falls deeper in love
with Will. Crossing over would give Kathy the freedom to do
whatever she wanted with her magic. No rules. No limitations. It
would also mean breaking the bond she has always shared with her
sister, who has made it clear that she wants nothing to do with the
dark side.

When Will proposes they take over the underworld, Kathy loves the
idea of having power. But it also leaves her with a choice that will
change her life: abandon her family and the life she has always
known, or give up the love of her life forever.

More by the author

To find more books by the author, visit
DavidNethBooks.com/Books

* * *

Subscribe to his newsletter to be the first to know of new
releases and special deals!
DavidNethBooks.com/Newsletter

* * *

If you enjoyed the book, please consider leaving a review
on Goodreads or the retailer you bought it from. Reviews
help potential readers determine whether they'll enjoy a
book, so any comments on what you thought of the story
would be very helpful!

About the author

David Neth is the author of the Coven series, the Under the Moon series, Heat series, the Fuse series, and other stories. He lives in Batavia, NY, where he dreams of a successful publishing career and opening his own bookstore.

Also writes small town romance as D. Allen.

www.DavidNethBooks.com

www.facebook.com/DavidNethBooks

Made in the USA
Monee, IL
28 September 2021

78402245R10142